NOLA STREET TALES

VENGEANCE

PART TWO

A Novel by

E. Nigma

Copyright © 2020 Kevin Casey

Published by Major Key Publishing

www.majorkeypublishing.com

ALL RIGHTS RESERVED.

Any unauthorized reprint or use of the material is prohibited. No part of this book may be reproduced or transmitted in any form or by any means, electronic, or mechanical, including photocopying, recording, or by any information storage without express permission by the publisher.

This is an original work of fiction. Names, characters, places and incidents are either products of the author's imagination or are used fictitiously and any resemblance to actual persons, living or dead is entirely coincidental.

Contains explicit language & adult themes suitable for ages 16+

To submit a manuscript for our review,

email us at

submissions@majorkeypublishing.com

This is the continuance of the NOLA Street Tales Saga. Please check out part one (The Rise of Sharice) if you haven't yet.

Dedicated to anyone who had a close friend who betrayed you and broke your heart. Forgive, but never forget.

Chapter 1

Vulnerability

In her office, after a late and long night, Sharice was behind her desk sleep, recovering from the drinking she had done the prior night. Leaned back in her chair and covered with a jacket, with her feet kicked up on her desk, Sharice slept peacefully when suddenly her office door opened. Jerome walked in, noticed his old love fast asleep, and quietly closed her office door, making his way beside her.

He admired her beauty and reminisced about their time together when they were a couple. He noticed her legs as well, which always was his favorite feature of her. His eyes really lit up when he noticed her feet as a devious smile entered his face. Sharice always had pretty feet because she kept her toes pedicured at all times. He quietly made his way by her feet, and after several moments, he lightly tickled her.

It doesn't take long for Sharice to awaken from her slumber. She jumped up confused when she noticed Jerome, who stood by her, laughing.

"Jerome? What the fuck are you doing here?" a confused Sharice asked.

"I never heard from you about dinner, so I decided to pay you a visit," he said as Sharice calmed down.

"Dinner? Nigga, we just spoke last night!" Sharice exclaimed as she sat back in her chair, putting on her heels.

"I know, you took too long," Jerome responded as he took a seat across from her.

"How did you even get in here?" Sharice asked.

"Tracy let me in. Said it was time for you to get up

anyway. Look, are you gonna sit here and do this twenty questions shit, or are you gonna let me take you out?" Jerome questioned while Sharice checked the time on her cell phone.

"It's like one o'clock. Kinda early for dinner, isn't it?" she responded.

"Well, I figure we can grab a bite to eat early, talk, and then spend the rest of the afternoon deciding on what to eat for dinner," Jerome said with a slick grin.

Sharice sighed as she wiped her eyes.

"I can't do all that. I'm in the same clothes I wore last night," she explained. "I need to shower, get a change of clothes, and do some other shit, so that's not gonna work for me."

"Tracy said you have a whole wardrobe in your office, and there's a shower downstairs. She also said that your schedule is open as far as she's aware," Jerome said with a smile.

Sharice frowned and shook her head.

"Tracy's about to be unemployed if she keeps

tellin' all my business," Sharice said as Jerome laughed.

"Come on, Kiss. Get ready. It'll be fun. You look like you could use the break," he said.

Sharice took a deep breath before she agreed.

"Fine, fuck. You're a pushy muthafucka, I swear," Sharice said as she got up from her chair and motioned Jerome to leave her office. "Alright, get out. Wait for me downstairs."

Jerome agreed as he made his way out of the office. Sharice reached in her desk drawer for her toothbrush and toothpaste as she headed out of the office as well. She made her way to the downstairs bar area, where Tracy was overseeing a liquor delivery. Sharice made her way over to her friend, and Tracy noticed the look in her friend's eye.

"Don't give me that look. Your ass need to get out of the office and have some fun," Tracy said as Sharice gave her the evil eye. "Now, gone on, don't keep your date waiting. Gone on!"

Sharice frowned as Tracy shooed her away before she finally made her way to the back bathroom. Tracy giggled as she went back to working on her inventory.

A little under an hour later, Sharice reappeared well-groomed, fresh, and in full makeup, wearing a form-fitting sundress. Jerome was sitting at the bar conversing with Tracy when he noticed Sharice making her way towards them. He jumped up from his barstool, impressed as he approached his date.

"Shit, I was wondering what was taking so long. Now I see it was worth the wait," Jerome said as he checked her out.

Sharice rolled her eyes with a smirk on her face before she turned her attention towards Tracy.

"Is anyone here?" she asked.

"Michelle. She's upstairs waiting for James to come by," Tracy answered.

"Can you go get her for me real quick?" Sharice

asked, which caused Tracy to shoot her a look.

"Yes'm, master, let me gone get her fer' you," Tracy mocked with a deep southern accent while walking off.

Sharice giggled at her friend's actions before she turned to Jerome, who is mesmerized with her beauty.

"Damn, I forgot how beautiful you are," he said.

"Well, if you came around more often instead of when you want something, you wouldn't have forgotten," Sharice snapped.

She loved the fact that the roles are reversed. The previous night, he caught her off guard and had her undivided attention. Now, she's turned the tables and owned him, drunk with her beauty.

As Jerome looked over his date, Michelle and Tracy made their way back downstairs as Michelle checked out her boss as well.

"Well damn, ain't you lookin' nice," she said when she noticed Sharice's sundress. "Almost makes me wanna go dyke."

Sharice chuckled as Michelle turned her attention to Jerome.

"Almost," she said. "You must be the one that has her all dressed up at two in the afternoon. And you are?"

"None of your business," Sharice snapped as Michelle laughed.

"My bad, boss, my bad. Just making conversation."

Sharice shook her head and turned her attention to Jerome.

"Hey, can you wait outside? I need holla at my girl for a minute," Sharice said.

Jerome nodded before he made his way out of the club. Tracy walked back to the bar as Sharice led Michelle over to an empty table.

"Look, I didn't mean to disrespect you back there, I was only joking," Michelle said.

"Girl, I'm not worried about all that," Sharice

replied. "You know where Bull is?"

"No. I heard he was going out with a few of his Guido friends to celebrate a wedding, bachelor party, or whatever the fuck they do, but outside of that, I don't know," Michelle answered. "A little early for that, I would think."

"You don't know the Italians," Sharice responded. "I want you to give him a call. Tell him that me and Connie are going to the hairdresser tomorrow morning at nine. He should know which one, but if he asks, the one on St. Bernard. Just say I wanted him to know where we would be tomorrow."

Michelle was confused but nodded her head.

"Keep this shit between us. Nobody needs to know," she ordered.

"Alright. I got you. Everything alright?" Michelle asked.

"I guess I'll see. Leave tomorrow morning open," Sharice said. "Oh, and one more thing, Michelle. Don't fuck with my man."

Sharice looked serious initially, but eventually, a smirk entered her face as Michelle nodded her head, acknowledging the joke.

"Well, I hope you have a nasty time today," she replied.

Sharice burst into laughter before she walked off.

As soon as Sharice left, Michelle pulled out her phone and dialed Bull as instructed.

Bull, Ritchie, and several other Faction Italian members was all drinking after a wedding as they watched the bride and groom dance together. The wedding hall was packed with people dressed in their expensive suits and dresses. There were two big tables of food laid out as kids ran around the hall playing. There's also a live band who entertained the wedding guests.

Bull laughed and joked with his table crew when his cell phone suddenly rang. He answered the call and was confused by what he heard.

"What... The hairdresser?... Okay, and you're telling me this why?... Okay... fine, yeah... alright," he said as he hung up the phone.

Ritchie overheard Bull's conversation and questioned him.

"You gettin' calls about hairdressers now?" he playfully asked.

"I swear, I will never understand Sharice even after all these years," Bull responded.

"What happened?"

"What, you wanna hear this?" Bull asked.

"I'm curious."

"The new girl, Michelle, calls me up and tells me Sharice and Connie are going to the hairdresser tomorrow morning like I need to know that shit. Crazy, huh?" Bull said to a confused Ritchie.

"So, you're their driver now?"

"No, she just wanted me to know about it. Like I don't have other things to worry about," Bull answered.

After he heard that bit of information, Ritchie continued digging.

"What hairdresser?"

"Huh?"

"What hairdresser does she go to?" Ritchie asked.

"Why? You lookin' to set an appointment?" Bull joked with his friend.

"My goomar, she's looking for a new spot since her last guy up and moved. Sharice is a piece of ass and always has nice hair. Maybe they can work their magic on her," Ritchie quickly explained.

Bull looked at Ritchie strangely before he answered his question.

"It's a spot off St. Bernard Avenue. Don't know the name of it, but it's on the corner of St. Bernard and Paris. Let me say this, I don't think all the hairdressers in the world can make your goomar look like Sharice. They just do hair, remember?" Bull joked, driving Ritchie to laughter.

"You'd be surprised what a good wig would do,

my friend," Ritchie replied.

He and Bull joked with each other while Ritchie smiled, knowing this bit of information.

In an upscale restaurant on Tchoupitoulas, Sharice and Jerome are lead to a private booth by their host. The atmosphere is pricey, with grand chandeliers located throughout the building. A pianist located in the center of the restaurant played tunes for the upscale clientele.

As they arrived at their table, Sharice cut Jerome off as she took the seat facing the entrance of the restaurant. Jerome smiled as he took the seat across from her. The host handed them their menus and explained the specials before walking off, leaving the two old flames alone.

Sharice was quietly looking over her menu, impressed while Jerome looked at her as if he's obsessed.

"Same ol' Kiss I see," he said, breaking the silence.

"What?"

"Always gotta have to door facing seat," he answered.

"I'm in the middle of a war," Sharice explained before correcting herself. "Well, I think I am. I don't really know, if I'm being truthful."

"You think them street niggas gonna come through here lookin' for you," Jerome asked before their waitress walked over and introduced herself.

She took both of their drink orders and made her way off as Sharice turned her attention back toward her date.

"Niggas, even the street ones, can surprise you," Sharice said with a smile. "Speaking of which, I'm surprised with you suggesting this spot. I half thought you were gonna bring me to Burger King or some shit!"

Jerome laughed as the waitress returned with their drinks and took their orders before leaving the lovers alone once again.

"Girl, you know you used to love that Burger King back in the day," Jerome said as Sharice took a sip of her drink.

"Yeah, made my ass fat fuckin' with you," she replied.

"And look at you now."

Sharice rolled her eyes, smirking. Jerome's words always made her feel herself.

"So, why are we here?" she asked.

"Just to catch up, see how's life been treatin' you," he said.

"So, you not tryin' to fuck? That's good to know," Sharice said, which caused Jerome to spit up his drink.

His reaction caused Sharice to laugh while he gathered himself.

"I'm glad I can still get it out of you," she said.

"Come on now, Kiss. You know what happened to us wasn't on me. You decided to walk away, remember?" Jerome reminded her.

"I know, I know. Must you remind me of that shit every time we get together?"

"Yes, because just like last time, and every time going forward, I'm gonna try and get back with you," Jerome said.

Sharice tried to ignore him before she responded.

"Come on, Rome. I'm on the cusp of finally achieving my boss goal. I don't have time for romance and shit like that," Sharice explained.

"Whatever, Kiss," Jerome fired back. "You know good and well you could make this shit work if you wanted to. I mean, hell, look at the current bosses. Both Rico and John are married with families. In John's case, I believe he has grandchildren. Mike is... well, Mike is Mike, but you get what I'm sayin'."

"It's different for women, Rome, you know that," Sharice responded. "We don't have the luxury y'all do. It's like that old thing where in high school, if niggas fucked a bunch of women, he was a playa. If a woman did the same shit, she was a hoe. Ain't nothing changed. Being married, or in a relationship, makes us look weak like we need a man to survive."

Jerome laughed at Sharice's rationale.

"Bullshit," he replied. "You just hate being locked down. I don't know what it is, but you're scared of being tied down. I mean, you always was like that."

"No, I was not. It has nothing to do with that," Sharice fired back.

"Kiss, please," Jerome quipped to a smirking Sharice. "Name one nigga you then been with longer than me. Just one!"

Sharice pondered for a moment before responding.

"Doesn't mean anything. Any nigga I was with after you was for fun, nothing else. They didn't mean shit like..." Sharice said before pausing. "It's nothing like what you think it is."

"What was you about to say?" Jerome asked while Sharice waved him off. "Nah, finish that statement! They didn't mean shit, like what?"

"Anyway, moving on. I---"

"No, I want you to finish that statement," Jerome demanded.

Sharice sat silent, taking a few sips of her drink.

"You can't even say how you feel about me, can you?" Jerome asked.

Sharice remained quiet once again. Jerome shook his head with disappointment.

"I don't know why you make me do this to you, but so be it," he said to a confused Sharice.

"Do what to me?" she asked before Jerome quickly reached under the table and grabbed one of Sharice's ankles, almost pulling her out of her seat.

He quickly removed her heel from her foot as Sharice looked around, terrified.

"Are you out of your fuckin' mind?" she quietly said. "Don't do this, Rome, please!"

"Admit it. You're still in love with me, aren't you?" Jerome said.

Sharice frowned at him, not wanting to give in to

her old love.

"Jerome, this shit ain't funny, now let me go! I'm not playin'-" Sharice said before she let out a loud yelp as Jerome started tickling her foot.

Sharice covered her mouth, trying to contain herself as other customers started to look toward their way. Jerome stopped tickling his victim as Sharice tried to gather herself.

"Jerome! Please don't do this. I'm begging you," Sharice pleaded while she tried to wrestle her ankle away from Jerome's tight grip to no avail.

"Come on, Kiss, let me hear it. You still love me, don't you?" Jerome asked with a sadistic grin.

"Rome, please don't! I can't take-"

"Wrong answer," Jerome said while he tickled the arch of Sharice's foot once again.

Sharice reacted with a loud cackling laugh, which delighted her tormenter. Jerome was relentless while Sharice was almost in tears. He stopped his onslaught when one of the waiters made their way over.

"Sir, do we have a problem?" he said while Sharice attempted to wrestle her foot away.

"No, it was just a real funny joke. Our apologies," Jerome said while keeping his hold of Sharice's ankle concealed under the secluded table.

"Well, can you please lower your tone?" the waiter said. "There are others here trying to enjoy their meals."

Jerome nodded his head as the waiter hurried off. He turned his attention back to Sharice, who was recovering from Jerome's last tickle attack.

"Now, we both know I've been taking it easy on you right now," Jerome said. "Now, if you don't want me to get to those toes, and have you acting a fool until we both get kicked out of this bitch, tell me what I want to hear."

A defeated Sharice finally gave in to Jerome as she slowly nodded her head.

"I still love you," she said much to the pleasure of Jerome.

"See, was that hard?" Jerome said with a smile.

Sharice tried to lower her leg, but Jerome still kept a firm grasp of her ankle, which confused her.

"Rome, what are you doing? I told you what you wanted to hear, fuck," she said.

"I wonder. Do you still get going when someone touches that spot?" Jerome teased as fear shot in the eyes of Sharice once more.

Before she can respond, Jerome began rubbing her on the side of her foot ever so gently. Sharice initially fought it but gave up struggling, giving in to his touch. She began breathing heavily when a state of bliss filled her face.

"I knew it. Kiss, you ain't changed one bit," Jerome said as he had total control of Sharice. "So, I guess the question is, my place or yours?"

Jerome intensified his touch on the side of her foot, which caused Sharice to slightly moan.

"Mines," Sharice answered as Jerome finally released her foot.

Much to his surprise, Sharice didn't pull her leg away from him as he stroked her spot, much to her enjoyment.

The two were surprised when the waitress returned to their table with their food and noticed Sharice's mood. She looked at Jerome, who smiled.

"Yeah, we're gonna need to get that to go, please," Jerome said to the waitress, who nodded her head and took the food back to prep it to go.

Sharice looked at Jerome, who smiled at her while he kept her in the mood by working her secret spot driving her wild.

About an hour later, Sharice and Jerome have finished their meal in Sharice's dining room. Jerome topped off Sharice's wine glass as she shot him a look.

"Really, nigga?" Sharice stated, already tipsy. "You trying to get me drunk, drunk."

"Kiss, you know the routine. First, I get you drunk, then we head up to your bedroom, and handle our business. Sober sex with you is difficult as fuck to deal with," Jerome said as he took a sip of his wine glass.

Sharice looked offended by his comment until a smile eventually grew on her face.

"So, you trying to say I'm difficult to please?" she questioned.

"Nah, I ain't saying all that. It's just you like to control shit. You don't know how to just lay back and take the dick," Jerome said, which caused Sharice to laugh.

"I know how to lay back and take it!" Sharice snapped.

"Bull shit," Jerome responded. "When I used to go down on you back in the day, you kept pulling back, trying to control shit. Here my dumb ass is trying to wear that shit out, and you squirming like a bitch cause you wanna do it your way."

Sharice chuckled while she reminisced for a moment.

"That wasn't why I was pulling back," she admitted. "It was just feeling so good, I didn't want it to end. I was trying to keep it going as long as I could. You just don't know what that was doing to me."

Jerome was surprised by her explanation.

"Well, shit," he said with a chuckle. "You should have let me work it then. I wouldn't have stopped even if you came. Just working this tongue over and over again until there was no fight left in you."

His words caused Sharice to giggle. The very thought of him going down on her turned her on. Sharice slowly rose from her chair and sat on Jerome's lap. She kissed him as her body begged for him. After a few moments, Jerome rose from his chair with Sharice in his arms. He slowly navigated his way towards Sharice's bedroom.

Once there, he laid Sharice gently onto her bed, quickly reached under her sundress and removed her panties. He left her heels on for the moment as he lifted her dress exposing her mid-section. He quickly began to run his tongue on her womanhood, which instantly sent Sharice into a state of bliss. Every stroke of Jerome's tongue drove Sharice wild as she began moaning loudly.

After a few moments, the mood suddenly changed for Sharice as she tried to stop Jerome's advances.

"Jerome, wait! Please stop," she said.

Jerome ignored her as he continued to lick her, keeping his promise on not backing down this time. Sharice finally rolled to the side once she was finally released from Jerome's grasp. He looked at her with confusion as she got up from the bed.

"Reese, what's wrong?" he asked.

"I'm sorry, Rome... I... I can't do this," Sharice said. "Please, could you just leave?"

Jerome was confused as he rose from the bed and approached her. Sharice waved him off while she backed away.

"Was it something I did," he asked.

"No, it's not you. It's just... please leave, Jerome. I can't do this," Sharice answered.

Jerome was still confused but honored her wishes as he made his way out of Sharice's home. Sharice walked to her bathroom with tears streaming from her eyes.

"What the fuck is wrong with me?" she questioned as she wiped the tears from her face.

She looked in the mirror for a moment and sighed before making her way back to her bedroom.

Later that night, Connie and Agent Flores, under her Rose guise, were in Connie's apartment having just finished a sexual encounter before Rose walked into the bathroom to clean up a bit. Connie's apartment was spacious, with limited furniture. Most of her belongings are still boxed up even though she'd been living there for about a year.

Connie, who was nude, rolled over to the side of

the bed, located her underwear, and put them back on before locating a blunt and her lighter. She lit up the blunt and took a puff while she fiddled with the lighter in her hand. Rose exited the bathroom and immediately began fanning the smoke in the room.

"Girl, put that shit out. They check piss at my job," Rose said as Connie shrugged her off.

"I got a piss guy, don't sweat it," she said as she took a few more puffs and offered it to Rose, who refused.

"I'm serious, girl. I don't like all that shit. Please. For me," Rose said as she walked over and slowly rubbed Connie's tattoo- filled legs.

Connie smiled, nodding her head. She took one last puff before she put the blunt out on a nearby ashtray on her nightstand.

"I must like you, chica, 'cause I don't put out the blunt for no bitch," Connie said.

"Bullshit. You love me, mami," a seductive Rose said before she worked her way up Connie's body, kissing her passionately.

After several more kisses, Rose turned to the side and grabbed her phone from the nightstand when she noticed Connie's taped up Smith and Wesson revolver gun on the floor.

"Hey, I've been meaning to ask you, what kind of work do you do?" she asked Connie, who still was fidgeting with her lighter.

"I own a few businesses here and there," Connie said. "Why, you looking for work?"

"No, I just saw the gun down there and wanted to know what you did, that's all," Rose responded.

Connie looked down at the gun and chuckled as she got comfortable on the bed.

"Just for protection. Niggas be wildin' out around here," she explained.

"Come on, Connie, I have brothers," Rose said. "Nobody tapes off a gun for protection. Seems like it's a little more than that."

Connie smiled as she turned to Rose.

"Well, in my line of business, you never know if or when you're gonna have to put someone down. It can be dangerous out there," she responded.

Rose nodded with understanding as she laid her head on Connie's lap. She noticed the lighter Connie was fidgeting with looked like a military lighter normally used by soldiers.

"Badass lighter. Where'd you get it?" Rose asked.

Connie chuckled as she looked at the lighter in her hand while she flipped the lid open and close repeatedly.

"This was my dad's," Connie said. "The only thing I have from him. Well, other than my looks, I guess since I didn't look much like my mom."

"What, did he leave you?"

"Well, in a certain way, I guess you could say that," Connie answered. "He got put away for some murder shit back in the day when I was like five or something. I don't even remember him."

"Damn, sorry to hear that. You ever thought

about going to see him?" Rose asked.

"Nah, he died a while back. My junkie ass mom didn't worry about it when I was young, so I missed my chance to ever really see him," Connie said, dropping her hardcore demeanor for a moment.

"Shit, Mami," Rose responded. "Your mom still around?"

"Died of an overdose when I was like fifteen. It didn't matter 'cause the state took me out her house long before that."

"In and out of group homes, I'm guessin'. Right?" Rose questioned.

"Yeah, how you know?" Connie responded.

"You don't seem like the type that stays still, for real," she replied, causing Connie to laugh.

"Nah, I guess not. I don't regret life, you know. It made me who I am, so I can't complain. Shit coulda been a lot worse."

Rose smiled while she kissed Connie's inner thigh softly.

"My roughneck, Mami," she said.

Connie smiled as she placed her lighter on the nightstand.

"I can tell you're different than other bitches I then fucked with," Connie said.

"How so?"

"I don't never talk about my past with anyone. Most bitches just like to smoke and fuck. You actually listenin' and shit. Hell, I don't think even Sharice knows the full story," Connie responded.

"Sharice? Is she like your ex or something?" Rose asked.

Connie burst into laughter.

"Nah, just a friend. Coulda been the one, you know. She just didn't see it in me though. Claim she all straight and shit, then I found out she fucked one of our friends we grew up with. You think you know people," Connie said as she looked at an attentive Rose. "My bad, I'm sitting here boring you with my shit."

"No, I like hearing about you. Let's me see who you really are," Rose responded to a smiling Connie. "So you and Sharice, is that over?"

"It'll never be over with us," Connie said. "We're business partners, although she treats me like I'm the help half the time. If it wasn't for me, she wouldn't have got where she is. Pisses me off sometimes."

"I know the feeling. I had a friend who I helped get supervisor at my old job, and then the bitch wanted to act all high and mighty. Like she wasn't with us back in the day," Rose said.

Connie nodded her head with agreement.

"You see, that's what I'm sayin'. You put in work with them, and as soon as they move up, they treat you like you're fuckin' stupid. Her sleepin' with Lavina though, that shit was wrong. It was a fuckin' betrayal, I swear. To tell the truth, I'm actually glad she's hurt about that shit," vented Connie.

"Hurt? Why, what happened?" Rose asked.

Connie chuckled once more as she shook her

head.

"Life, Rose. That's what happened," she responded while she fondled with Rose's breasts. "Anyway, enough of my fucked-up life. You ready for round two?"

Rose smiled, rising from Connie's lap to mount her.

"The question is, are you ready," she replied while she leaned in and began kissing her mark.

She slowly began making her way down Connie's body, making sure she kissed and licked every spot that gets a reaction. Connie was filled with pleasure from her lover.

Hours later, Rose noticed Connie was asleep and quietly got out of bed. She tiptoed around the room as she picked up the gun she noticed earlier, and the lighter Connie had left on the nightstand. She grabbed her phone as well and snuck into the bathroom.

Once she's in the bathroom, she began taking several pictures of the gun and the lighter from multiple angles. She sent the photos out via email, and once the email notified her the message had been sent, she deleted the pictures from her phone.

She peeked her head out of the bathroom and noticed Connie was still asleep. She once again tiptoed and returned the items back to their position before she made her way back towards the bed. She slid in quietly, going unnoticed before she wrapped her arms around Connie, finally going to sleep herself.

Back at club Exotica, Tracy walked into Sharice's office, turned on the light, and was startled to see a drunken Sharice sitting behind her desk with a glass in her hand.

"Shit! Girl, you scared the hell outta me," Tracy said as she walked over to her friend. "I didn't even see you come in. I thought you'd be out getting the dust knocked off your cooch."

"Pussy," Sharice corrected. "Dust knocked off my pussy. I'm not five years old, you can say pussy."

"Well, sorry, my motherly skills are just a habit. So why aren't you out getting the dust knocked off your pussy?" Tracy asked, taking a seat across from her friend.

Sharice struggled with her words as she finished her drink before deciding to respond.

"We started to, you know, get it together. It was nice, but all of a sudden, I told him to leave. I couldn't explain it, but it didn't feel right. It wasn't nothing he did, it's just... I don't know," Sharice tried to explain.

Tracy nodded her head with understanding.

"I guess I saw this coming. Doesn't surprise me actually," Tracy responded, confusing Sharice.

"What?"

"Sharice, you have a closed personality. Basically, you don't let anyone in or open up to anybody about anything, which is why you struggle with your love life," Tracy answered.

"Don't open up to anybody? I talk to you all the time," Sharice replied.

"Yeah, but you're not trying to fuck me," Tracy said with a smile. "My guess is you felt the situation getting too close for comfort and cut it off from there. I mean, even though you're in denial about Lavina, it's the same thing there. Opening up or connecting with someone sexually makes you feel vulnerable. You hate feeling vulnerable more than you like feeling loved, so you push folks away. If this was just a simple fuck, I think you'd been fine, but for people you actually care about, you shut it down before it can begin. Why are you so afraid to let yourself be loved?"

Sharice hesitated before she reached for a bottle on her desk to refill her glass, but was blocked as Tracy snatched the bottle away.

"Answer the question," Tracy commanded.

Sharice sighed as she pondered for a few seconds.

"I don't know, I guess I have goals and shit. I'm on the cusp of gettin' where I finally wanna be! I can't risk it all for a nigga. Not right now. I'm so close, Tracy, you have no idea. Love is just a distraction," Sharice answered to an unmoved Tracy.

"So this is it, huh? This is all you're strivin' for? To be the top bitch in your thing?" Tracy mocked. "Sharice, there's so much to life outside of power and money. By the time you realize it, it'll be too late. Guys like Jerome won't wait around. You keep it up, and you're going to have all the money and power in the world, but nobody to share it with. Is that how you wanna end up?"

Sharice became a little emotional as Tracy's words rang true to her.

"How... how can I change?" Sharice struggled to ask her friend. "I don't know what to do."

"You can have both things, Sharice, but you have to allow yourself to be vulnerable. That's what relationships are all about. Put your faith in him. No man would keep coming around if he didn't see something he loves. Trust me," Tracy responded. "I saw this on a show once where one character was asking another character about advice on life, and he responded with 'You only have one life, do it all.' He's right, do it all. It helped that his character was a billionaire, so it's easy for him to say that, but the advice is still real."

Sharice chuckled as Tracy rose from her seat.

"Look, you're in no condition to drive. Let me get with Lee and let him know he's closing the club tonight, and I'll drive you home. You don't need to sleep here again," Tracy said.

Sharice nodded with agreement while Tracy walked out of the office. Sharice pulled out her cell phone and looked up Jerome's number. She's about to press the call button, when she stopped at the last moment and exited from her contact list. Sharice, still an emotional mess, slowly rose from her desk and prepared to leave for the night.

Chapter 2

Trust

The next morning, Sharice woke up in her bed, groggy as she checked the time on her cell phone on a nearby nightstand. She held her head from the throbbing pain she was having from the aftereffect of drinking the previous night before she located her remote and cut on her TV.

She wiped her eyes and nestled back into her bed as she checked her phone. Eventually, she had gone to Jerome's contact and was about to call, but as she had done the night before, she resisted. This time, however, she did text him with a simple message of:

Hey.

As she watched the news, she received a text back from Jerome:

Hey.

Sharice smiled as she texted back.

Can I see you today?

She waited for a response wondering was she being too forward. Eventually, Jerome responded.

Sure, you want me to come by now?

Sharice chuckled as she texted him.

Meet me at the club round one.

Jerome responded.

Bet

Satisfying Sharice, who had a big smile on her face.

Her smile was short lived as a news story on the TV caught her attention. She quickly turned up the volume. The story was about a drug bust of a container from Columbia on the docks that occurred overnight. Sharice was annoyed as she texted both Bull and Connie to meet her at the club ASAP. She quickly jumped out of bed to get dressed.

Outside of a local downtown beauty shop, Lil Dee, Eric, and another crew member are parked down the street looking around the area in anticipation of Connie and Sharice's expected arrival. Lil Dee seemed frustrated as boredom was overtaking him.

"Y'all niggas got me out here this early 'cause y'all dumb asses couldn't hit the right chick," Lil Dee said, aiming his comments toward Eric.

"Look, nigga, if you would have gave us a better description other than fine, we wouldn't have had to come back out here," Eric snapped back. "You think I wanna be out this bitch this early? Fuck!"

The two continued to go back and forth as Michelle, wearing a slutty scuffed up outfit walked down the sidewalk as if she's a dope fiend. She noticed the crew sitting in the car, observing the area. She did her best dope fiend act as she walked over to their car and knocked on the window, surprising the crew. She noticed the guns they were holding as Lil Dee lowered his window.

"What the fuck you want?" he said as Michelle began fiddling her hair.

"What's up, daddy? Can you spare me a few bucks, baby? Please," she said to a disgusted Lil Dee.

"Bitch, if you don't get yo' raggedy-ass from 'round me with that bullshit!" Lil Dee said.

"Please, daddy. Come on, I'll suck your dick, baby. I'll suck it real good," she said as Lil Dee cringed at the very thought of having sex with a dope fiend.

Michelle continued to be aggressive to the irritated crew. Lil Dee finally had enough as he went into his wallet and tossed a couple of dollars out the window.

"There! Now get the fuck outta here," he said.

"Thank you, baby," an excited Michelle said as she quickly scooped up the money and continued down the sidewalk.

Lil Dee rolled up the window as he and the others observed the area cautiously. After she was out of sight, Michelle stopped the fiend act and walked toward a payphone with a smirk on her face.

In Sharice's club office, Sharice, Connie, and Bull were meeting while Sharice looked for answers from her crew.

"How am I finding out about this from the fuckin' news and not you two?" fussed Sharice from behind her desk. "I mean, seriously? I thought you all had everything taken care of out there!?"

"We do, it's just... I don't know... Maybe the feds moved in so fast that our connect didn't have a chance to respond," Bull said.

"This is why I don't like movin' dope on those docks! Now the feds are gonna be all up in our shit for the rest of the fuckin' year over this shit," Sharice said as she grabbed her head in frustration. "One of y'all reach out to Duvan, Duval, or whatever the fuck his name is and apologize for the inconvenience. Let him know the next shipment is on me."

Bull and Connie were silent as Sharice noticed how quiet they had become.

"What?"

"Well, there's a problem. We kinda... well... we guaranteed their shipment," Connie said to an enraged and shocked Sharice.

"Are you fuckin' kidding me?" Sharice growled while she rose from her chair and approached both Connie and Bull. "You guaranteed a fuckin' drug shipment?! Are you out of your fuckin' minds?! Do you have enough green to cover this shit?"

Connie shook her head as Sharice turned her attention to Bull.

"What about you?" she said. "You gotta grip to spare!?"

Bull didn't respond as Sharice shook her head in disbelief.

"Do you know what Columbians do to their

victims?" she asked. "It involves fire, screwdrivers, and saws, and trust me when I say they are very good at their jobs keepin' niggas alive to feel every portion of it! Now, I don't know what you have to say to that man, but you need to fix it! Come up with a payment plan, or work some shit out 'cause I can tell you one thing, it's y'alls muthafuckin' problem, not mine! Fix it!"

Bull and Connie both nodded their head and were about to make their way out of the office when Sharice called Connie back.

"Not you, Connie. You stay," she said as Bull made his way out of the office.

Sharice sat behind her desk and took out a couple of aspirin as Connie looked on as a child who was just scolded by a parent.

"What the fuck is wrong with you?" Sharice asked her friend before she took her aspirin. "I mean seriously, how could you fuck this up? I didn't even wanna do this shit, but you were all 'it's an easy score' and shit, and now you have us in a hole for millions?"

"I'm sorry, Reese. I wasn't thinkin'. I was just tryin' to close the deal and-"

"And pocket extra money for yourself without tellin' me," Sharice said as she cut off her friend. "I'm sure you got a good rate to guarantee the shipment. How many times I then told you, being greedy is gonna fuck you up! You gotta be smart! These niggas already think we're a fuckin' joke! Then you go out there and do some dumb shit and prove it!"

Sharice's words started to irritate Connie as she shot her a look.

"Don't put this shit all on me," she snapped back. "Don't forget, you the one who sanctioned this shit! You talk about me being greedy, but yo' ass just as greedy as me keepin' this shit from Money and the other bosses. Don't sit here and give me shit like it's all on me!"

Sharice sighed as she calmed down. Connie was right. Sharice was looking for a quick score, and against her better judgment, agreed to pull this job.

"Either way, you gotta be smart," Sharice responded. "Yeah, I was looking at a quick hit, but I have my limits. Making stupid decisions for money, we just can't do that."

Connie sighed as she took a seat across from her friend.

"So now what?" Connie asked.

"Now you sit down with the Columbian and make peace," Sharice responded. "Some shit you gonna have to face on your own."

Connie shook her head before Sharice's phone suddenly rang. She answered and listened to a message before hanging up her phone and pulling out another phone from her purse. She placed the battery in the phone and waited for it to load.

"Who was that?" a curious Connie asked.

"Michelle. I had her working on something for me," Sharice said as she dialed the number from her first phone onto the new one.

"Yeah, it's me. What you got?" she said.

Michelle was about a block down from the beauty shop, still looking down towards Lil Dee and crew in their car.

"Yeah, so there's a crew who's set up down the block. They gatted up and everything waiting to make a move," Michelle said.

Sharice sighed as her worst fears of Bull being the leak have come true.

"You recognize any of them?" she asked.

"Yeah, one of them," Michelle answered. "Lil Dee. Nigga then tried to fuck me several times back in the day. Surprised he didn't recognize me when I walked up on him."

"Never heard of him. Who's he with?"

"He runs with his cousin Dre. They own a few corners uptown. Sixth and Baronne is their money spot though," Michelle answered.

A stunned Sharice grabbed her head with frustration.

"I'll be damned," Sharice exclaimed. "Alright, peep them out for a little longer. See if Dre shows up. If they still there in about an hour, just roll out and meet me back at the club."

"Okay, I'm on it," Michelle said before she disconnected the line.

Sharice put down her phone and laughed in disbelief, confusing Connie.

"Yo, what's up?" Connie asked.

"Dre. It's muthafuckin' Dre," Sharice exclaimed. "That's the nigga trying to move against me. This ol' one-legged bitch ass nigga is tryin' to make a move on me!"

"Who?"

"The nigga I shot on the corner of Sixth and Baronne! Remember the one I shot in the knee?" Sharice said to Connie, who shrugged.

"Bitch, you was right there! You know what?

Never mind. Cut back on that shit, Connie, for real," Sharice said. "Them niggas will get theirs, but the more immediate issue is Bull is snitchin' us out!"

Connie was stunned with the news as Sharice leaned back in her chair.

"Reach out to Diego, get an update on that shooting outside the pool hall. Also, get any information he has about Dre. Where he lays his head, who else he runs with, all that. We need to nip this shit in the bud before it gets out of hand," Sharice said.

"Reese, Bull ain't like-"

"Connie, just do what I say," Sharice snapped back. "I ain't happy about this shit either, but who else could it be?"

"You owe him a chance to explain. You owe him that much," Connie fired back.

Sharice pondered her decision before she nodded with agreement.

"Fine. I want everyone back tonight after you

speak with the Columbian. Connie, he don't say some shit I wanna hear..." Sharice said, hinting on what may need to happen.

Connie nodded her head as she headed out of the office. Sharice shook her head once again in frustration.

Agents Daniels, Davis, and Flores were all looking at the pictures of Connie's gun and cigarette lighter that was obtained the night before at their hidden diner safe house. Agent Daniels shrugged as he continued to look at the pictures.

"I don't know. Seems too much of a risk," Daniels said.

"Where's the risk?" Flores asked. "I'll swap out the piece while she's sleeping with a replica. We take the original gun, run the ballistics to see if we get lucky, and swap it back out before she's any wiser."

Davis and Daniels looked at each other, both concerned.

"The problem is most of what you do won't work in court for us," Daniels responded. "The second you slept with your target throws everything out of the window."

"I had no choice," Flores fired back. "There have been plenty of court cases where an undercover agent has slept with their mark and still get convictions. Even if you don't use my testimony, if we find something, we make the swap back, you can bust her, and bring her in on the charge."

"And what if she uses the FBI gun to commit a crime?" Davis asked.

"We put blanks in there. I don't know. Come on, y'all. Work with me here. This is a good plan. I don't think she's dumb enough to carry a gun with bodies on it, but at least we can have it on file," Flores responded as she tried to plead her case.

Davis looked at Daniels, who shrugged.

"Tell me about the lighter again," Daniels asked as he looked at a photo of it.

"Simple, we're going to need a warrant to bug her lighter," Flores said. "The only way you can get a bug in Sharice's office is to bring a bug in and out. Connie carries this lighter everywhere. It's special to her, trust me. We could even attach a tracker to it if we wanted."

"No, a bug is one thing, but the judge isn't going to go for a tracker," Davis said. "And if we write it up, the judge is only going to allow us to use the bug when we know she's in Sharice's office. Remember, she's the real target here."

Daniels pondered his options for a moment as he looked at the lighter design. He took a look at Flores and nodded his head with approval.

"Okay, get the paperwork going. I'll send this off to the main office and let them start searching for the model of the lighter to see if we can even do it," Daniels said.

"Make sure any alterations don't hinder her ability to refill it," Flores warned. "It's sentimental, so it may be our only way to hear what's inside of that office. Also, do you have my cover apartment set up?"

"Yeah, just got the paperwork back today. They will have it wired in the next few hours," Davis said.

"Okay, great. I was thinking of inviting her over to my place tonight, so I can have some eyes when I'm making the switch on the gun," Flores said.

"That's a good idea," Daniels said as he turned his head to Davis. "Make sure they get on that ASAP. I'd like to have eyes on this and make sure support is on standby. We'll do the same once we're approved for the lighter."

Flores nodded her head in agreement as she made her way over to a computer and began working on her paperwork. Daniels chuckled as he looked at the picture lighter once more, studying it.

Connie was driving down a local back road when flashing police lights filled her view. She calmly pulled off to the side as the police vehicle followed her. Diego exited the vehicle and walked over to Connie's vehicle. She lowered the window waiting for his arrival.

"License and insurance please," Diego said as Connie rolled her eyes.

"Nigga, can you stop fuckin' around?" Connie said as Diego smirked. "My girl wants an update on that shootin' over by the pool hall. What you got?"

"Nothing really. They weren't connected to anybody. Well, one has an uncle who was charged in the late nineties, but outside of that, seems like a case of mistaken identity," Diego said. "Just some crazy shit about being in the wrong place at the wrong time."

Connie nodded her head as she thought silently for a moment.

"Aight, check it out. There's some niggas who run the corners at Sixth and Barrone, a nigga named Dre. Need you to find out whatever you can about this fool. Who he runs with, where he lays his head, shit like that," Connie said.

"Alright. I'll reach out to one of my uptown contacts. He a problem?"

"For now, he is. Won't be for much longer," Connie said as she pulled out an envelope and handed it to Diego.

"Okay, I'll get on it. Now, license and insurance," he responded to a confused Connie.

"Shit ain't funny," she replied.

"Yeah, but if someone is watching us, and ask me why I pulled you over, I can pass a detector test saying failure to use your blinker. You really need to work on that," Diego responded to a frustrated Connie, who reached for her ID.

"Yeah, because them watching you take that wad of cash won't raise any suspicions," a sarcastic Connie said as she handed her ID to Diego.

Diego chuckled as he looked over Connie's ID.

"Say, I almost forgot. My girl said you know something about a witness to our girl Lavina's murder. What can you tell me about it?" she inquired.

Diego looked at her strangely.

"What?"

"Lavina's murder. The one with the parlor that was robbed or whatever. She said y'all got a witness," Connie answered.

Diego handed Connie her ID back and is confused.

"Um... yeah, well... yeah, we have a girl who said she saw the suspect fleeing the crime. We're... we're going to meet with her when she returns from out of town the day after tomorrow to get what we can," Diego said, going with the story Sharice told him to relay to anyone who asked.

"Good, I hope y'all catch whoever did that shit," Connie said. "Thing is, my girl would like to have a word with her first. You got a address or something where we can hook up with her?"

Diego was stunned as he went into his wallet and

looked for the card Sharice gave her. He handed it to Connie, who took down the information.

"Thanks, love. You've been a good help. Glad we have niggas like you on the force," Connie mocked as she rolled up her window.

Connie sped off as Diego looked on with confusion, wondering what type of game was Connie playing.

Sharice was going through some paperwork, stressed in her office at the club when Jerome knocked on the door. He walked into the room with a smile on his face until he noticed she's stressing.

"Hey, you okay?" he asked as he took a seat across from her.

"No, I'm not," Sharice honestly admitted as she dropped the paperwork on her desk and leaned back in her chair. "Just one bullshit thing after another."

"Anything I can help with?" Jerome asked, causing Sharice to smile.

"No, I'm fine. I'll get through it," she answered. "Hey, I just wanted to apologize for yesterday. I didn't mean to get you up and going just to kick you out like that. It's just hard for me, that's all."

"Imagine how hard it was for me," Jerome joked, causing Sharice to chuckle with embarrassment.

"I'm so sorry about that," an apologetic Sharice said. "I'll make it up to you, I promise."

"How about spendin' the day with me?" Jerome suggested, catching his old lover off guard. "Me, and you, the lake. What do you say?"

Sharice sighed as she shook her head.

"Rome, really today is not a good day. I got so much shit going on right now that it ain't funny. I don't think I can-"

"Wasn't askin'," Jerome said with a smile. "You just said you owe me, so I'm not taking no for an answer."

Sharice sighed as she pondered for a moment.

"I guess I can get away for a while, but I gotta be

back here tonight. Meeting with the troops to handle some shit. I can't do the lake though. I'm kinda under fire right now," Sharice said. "Tell you what, you used to throw down in the kitchen back in the day. Why don't you hook me up with a little somethin' somethin'?"

Jerome laughed as he stood up from his seat.

"Oh, so now you want me to cook and shit?" he playfully asked. "That's gonna cost you. You ready to pay the penalty? Think long and hard before you answer."

Sharice rose from her chair as well as she approached Jerome. She pulled him in and kissed him, catching him off guard. After she was done, she backed away with a smile on her face.

"We'll see," she responded as she led an excited Jerome out of her office.

Outside a rundown hotel in the downtown area, Bull was sitting in a car across the street looking around the area when he noticed Connie, who made her way over to his car. The hotel he was monitoring was a dump, used mostly by people who wanted to go under the radar for whatever reason. Bull watched as a couple of homeless men dug through the hotel's dumpster looking for anything of value, which disgusted him.

Connie quickly got into the back seat as she looked at the hotel as well.

"Where the fuck you been?" Bull asked her.

"Had to take care of some shit for Sharice," Connie answered. "How's it looking out here?"

"As far as I can tell, he's still in there. You really wanna go through with this?" Bull asked.

"Nigga, do you got two-plus million to pay his ass?" Connie snapped back.

"Well no, but I thought we were supposed-"

"Then shut the fuck up. Unless you have a better plan, this is what we gonna go with," Connie said. "We'll just wait it out 'til dark, and take care of it.

Don't trip, I got this on lock, so we should be good."

Connie got comfortable as she laid down in the back of the car, much to Bull's surprise.

"The fuck is this?" he asked.

"I'm tired, shit. Had a long night," she answered.

"Oh, and I didn't?"

"We like cops and shit, nigga. It's a stakeout. I'll take the next watch and let you get some sleep if you want," Connie responded as she kicked off her tennis shoes causing Bull to frown.

"Mother of Christ, can you at least keep your shoes on," Bull asked.

"I'm tryin' to relax, fuck," Connie said with a smirk on her face.

Bull shook his head, disgusted as Connie snuck a peek at him. She smiled, but her mood quickly turned into concern as she thought about Sharice's words from earlier.

No way he's sellin' us out, Connie thought.

After a few moments, she closed her eyes to get

some rest.

Sharice was stuffing her face while Jerome looked on at her with a grin. The two were at Jerome's apartment in the dining room table next to each other. The apartment wasn't too flashy but was nicely decorated with several art pieces on display. His kitchen was adjacent to his dining area, which was updated with stainless steel appliances. There's plenty of natural light entering in with the massive windows that fill the area.

Jerome took a few bites of his food as Sharice pushed her empty plate away from her.

"Oh my god, that was so damn good," Sharice said while she licked her fingers. "Your ass always knew how to throw down. You put your foot in that shit, for real."

"Glad to see you still like my cookin'," Jerome responded as he pushed his plate toward her, offering his food.

"Nigga, you tryin' to get me fat?" Sharice questioned with a smile on her face.

"So you sayin' you don't want it?" he responded as he attempted to pull the plate back before Sharice blocked him.

"I didn't say all that," she said as she quickly finished the plate off.

Jerome chuckled as he attempted to collect the plates, but once again was blocked by Sharice.

"I got it, damn," she said as she gathered their plates. "It's the least I can do since you did all the cooking."

Jerome sat back and watched Sharice making her way to his sink. She started running water, placing the dishes in the sink. Jerome made his way over as well as she began washing the dishes and positioned himself behind her. He reached down under her skirt and surprised her as he worked his fingers down the crack of her backside.

"Boy, stop," Sharice said as she giggled.

"What?"

"I'm tryin' to clean up!"

"And I'm tryin' to get what you owe me," he responded.

Before Sharice can reply, Jerome quickly bent her over as Sharice grabbed hold of the edge of the sink. He removed her panties with a little assistance from his victim. He inserted himself in her, causing Sharice to gasp as she clutched the edge of the sink as tightly as she can. Each thrust sent pleasured Sharice more and more. She was on her tiptoes, in her heels, moaning.

"That's it! Tell me you love it! Tell me you love it!" Jerome said as he tried to break his lover, who fought him every step of the way.

Sharice refused to give him the satisfaction, remaining quiet with the exception of a moan or two. Jerome's onslaught became fiercer, and Sharice had no other choice but to give her tormentor what he wanted.

"I love it! I love it! I love it!" Sharice screamed in pleasure as Jerome continued to make sure she felt him for several more strokes.

After a few moments, Jerome removed his manhood from her backside, turned her around, and began to passionately kiss her. He led her to his bedroom as the two continued to make out the entire way.

Once in his room, he playfully pushed her on the bed, causing her to giggle as he lifted up her skirt. As he did during their last encounter the day before, he went down on her, running his tongue around her midsection, which drove her wild. Sharice almost pushed him away once more. She placed her hands on top of his head, but at the last second decided to let Jerome control her as she laid back and accepted the assault she received.

Sharice grabbed the headboard of the bed as she tried to fight off her orgasm as best she can. Her body arched as Jerome's tongue assault filled her with bliss. Her battle, however, was short lived. Sharice let out a deafening moan as she pulled the headboard as tightly as she could.

The onslaught continued making Sharice's legs shake out of control. Her body's sensitivity was through the roof. Jerome finished up when he noticed Sharice put up a little more resistance. He smiled as he made his way up and inserted his manhood, making the couple as one. He started to grind on her once he was in position and had Sharice driven wild once more.

Sharice had a smile on her face, because the release she received was long overdue. She wanted her lover to dominate her, just as he was doing. She deserved punishment for leaving him hanging the previous day and was willing to pay for her crime. Every pump of his body was warranted. She deserved this blissful torture and welcomed it.

Jerome switched up a bit as he lifted one of Sharice's legs up, almost bending it to her own head.

He removed the heel that was still on her foot and began licking on the side of her foot, which drove her wild. Jerome hitting her spot and grinding her was too much to handle, causing his victim's head to whip back and forth. As Jerome felt her body tensing up, he intensified his tongue on her foot, which caused her to have a second orgasm, this one stronger than the first. Jerome finished up shortly after, collapsing on the side of Sharice.

Both lovers were breathing heavily. Sharice looked a mess with her hair all over the place, and one heel on her foot. She giggled as she looked toward Jerome, who chuckled as well.

"Damn, girl, you must have been hella deprived," joked Jerome. "I thought that would take a little bit longer, for real."

"Fuck you," a playful Sharice responded while she kicked off her other heel and nestled her head into Jerome's chest as the two cuddled up.

"Can't blame you though. Good dick is hard to

find. Probably fuckin' with them little dick niggas," Jerome boasted.

"Negro, please. You always did think you was hot shit," Sharice fired back.

"Your ass thought I was too, didn't you?" Jerome said, poking Sharice in the side, causing her to burst into laughter in her weakened state. "Say I'm the shit!"

"Okay, okay, you're the shit! You're the shit," Sharice squealed out as Jerome ended his torture after a few more pokes.

"Man, this brings me back," Jerome said as he got a little more comfortable. "Remember when we first hooked up? Back around your prom. You was pissed off because ol' girl had asked me to the prom. I mean, we was broke up for like the tenth time that week, and since you didn't wanna go with me, I was like fuck it. Shit, what was that girl's name?"

"Shalonda Jefferson," a tired Sharice said.

"Shalonda! That's her! Damn, she was fine as

fuck," Jerome replied.

"She's fat as fuck now," Sharice pointed out. "She works at a bank on Canal. That girl looked like she ain't stopped eating since she left high school."

"Well, she was fine back then. I remember I came by your grandma's house, and you went hard as a bitch at me," Jerome said with a smile on his face. "That was also the same day I tickled the fuck out of you for the first time. You remember? You was givin' me all that attitude, and I had your ass crying in tears before I was done. Got under them arms and between them toes. Shit, it must have lasted an hour. Now, you can't even take five seconds. You gettin' old, Kiss. Kiss?"

Sharice had fell asleep on Jerome's chest as he admired her from above. He kissed her on her forehead, laid back, and reminisced on past encounters with Sharice.

Sharice was getting the rest she was never able to for the first time in a long time. She allowed someone to control her, and even though she felt vulnerable in his arms, she felt safer than ever.

Night time was upon the city and Bull was fast asleep behind the wheel of his car. Connie continued to observe the targeted hotel in silence when she suddenly received a text. She checked her phone and smiled as she tapped Bull on the shoulder to wake him.

"Yo, wake up. It's time," she said as she checked her gun.

"What? What happened?" Bull asked as he wiped his face.

"Three of them niggas pulled out. Only ones there is the one guarding his door, and the man himself. We need to jet though 'cause I don't know how much longer they gonna be gone," Connie said to a confused Bull.

"How do you know all this?" Bull questioned.

"Come on, we'll talk later," she responded as she

opened the door and made her way out of the car.

Bull hesitated, but eventually grabbed his gun and followed Connie to the hotel.

Once they've made their way in the hotel, they entered the elevator as Connie began to alter her attire to look more revealing. Bull couldn't help but notice Connie's body since he'd never really looked at her like that. Behind that rough exterior was a beautiful, sexy woman. much to his surprise.

"Okay, when we get up there, I'm gonna let you go around the corner and set up. I'm gonna distract him, you come up from behind, and knock that nigga out, ya dig?" Connie explained to Bull, who hadn't heard a word she said, obsessed over her.

Connie noticed Bull wasn't paying attention and snapped her fingers.

"Hello!" she yelled, snapping Bull out of his trance.

"Yeah, what?"

"Focus, nigga, damn. Go set up on the other side, and I'm gonna distract him. Knock his ass out, and try not to make too much noise. Don't wanna tip off the head nigga with these paper-thin walls," Connie said as he placed her gun in her pants on her backside.

"How you know this gonna work?" Bull asked.

"I just had you gazin', didn't I?" Connie said with a smirk.

Bull shrugged as the elevator door slowly opened.

Connie pointed him toward the right, as she made her way to the left. Once she hit the corner, she peeked around and noticed the bodyguard standing at attention just outside the target's door. Connie took a deep breath, put a smile on her face, and walked from behind the corner with a sexy sway. She approached the bodyguard and checked him out with a flirty look in her eyes.

"Hey, boo. You lookin' for some fun?" she said, grabbing the guard's attention.

The guard initially tried to avoid her, but eventually, she caught his attention as she tied up her shirt, really exposed her breasts.

"What are you doing here?" the guard asked in a heavy accent.

"Looking for you, sweet thang. I'm just trying to have some fun! What about you? You looking for some fun?" Connie said to the guard, who had turned his full attention towards her.

"So, you're a whore?" the guard asked her.

Connie smiled and shrugged.

"I'm whatever you want, baby," she said as she went closer, catching him off guard as she started rubbing on his midsection.

Bull came from the back and noticed the interaction. He paused as Connie shot him a quick look, wanting him to advance. Bull smiled as he continued to watch Connie entertain the guard. Connie became irritated but quickly smiled as the guard looked back towards her.

"You're very good," he replied. "My pants aren't even off, and you gave me a hard-on. So, how much is this gonna cost me?"

"Forty dollars, baby. Two dubs," Connie said.

The guard went into his pocket, pulled out a fifty, and handed it to a confused Connie.

"Here's a little extra. Make it count," the guard said as he unbuckled his pants. "I hope you're just as talented with your mouth as you were with your hand."

Connie was terrified as Bull watched on in amusement. She slowly dropped to her knees while Bull had enjoyed himself enough. He quickly made his way over and swung his gun, hitting the guard in the back of the head, and knocked him unconscious. His body fell on top of an irate Connie. She quickly jumped up with a frown on her face as she approached Bull.

"What the fuck was that?" she whispered.

"Oh, I didn't know you were ready for me," he

whispered back.

Connie was not amused as she unwrapped her shirt.

"You got the duct tape?" she asked.

"Yeah."

"Alright, let's move him to that utility closet down the hall."

Bull grabbed the top half of the guard as Connie grabbed his bottom half, and the two drug him off down the hall.

Several moments later, Bull and Connie returned to the hotel door, and Bull was about to kick the door in. Connie quickly stopped him, showing him a key to the door. Bull waved her forward as she quietly put the old-style key in the door and twisted it. She opened the door and breathed a sigh of relief that the inside lock wasn't applied. Both her and Bull entered the room quietly with their guns drawn out. They heard water running in the bathroom as Connie smiled and took a seat on the bed.

Duval made his way out of the bathroom and was stunned to see Connie sitting on the bed with her gun drawn at him. Bull also revealed himself after checking out the rest of the room. Duval's initial surprise quickly faded as he calmly looked around the room.

"The guy who was at my door. Is he dead?" he asked.

"Nah, not yet, but give it time, baby," Connie said with a wicked grin on her face.

"So, this is how you conduct business?" Duval replied. "My shipment is compromised, and you kill me as if I was the problem?"

"I don't know what to tell you. I'll admit I fucked up guaranteeing your shipment, but I didn't expect we'd have any issues. So if it makes you feel any better, this shit is all on me," Connie said before she rose from the bed.

"They warned me not to deal with niggers, but I wouldn't listen," Duval said with a scowl on his face.

"I see what you did there. Went with the hard R," Connie said with a smile on her face.

Duval sensed the end is near as he looked at both her and Bull.

"They won't let you get away with this. My people will come, and when they do, they are going to fuck you up," he said as an unbothered Connie shrugged.

"Well, that's why our president is building a wall," she mocked. "To keep people like you and yours outta here."

Before Duval can respond, Connie opened fire, landing several shots. She killed him as he quickly fell to the ground. She walked over towards his body and confirmed that he's dead before walking over toward Bull.

"Go kill the one in the closet so we can get the fuck outta here," Connie said as she quickly headed to the door. "Meet me at the lobby."

Bull was confused but followed instructions as he hurried down the hall to the utility closet.

As he made it down to the lobby area, he noticed Connie duct tapping the desk clerk to the chair. Bull was confused as he approached his friend.

"What the fuck are you doing?" Bull asked.

"Damn, took you long enough. Here, tape her other leg," Connie said, handing Bull the duct tape. Bull still didn't understand what was going on but complied as he began to tape the desk clerk, who wasn't putting up any resistance.

"Why are we leaving her to tell the story to the cops?" Bull asked.

"My bad. Tyronique, this is Bull. Bull, this is Tyronique," Connie replied as she finished taping her friend's leg. "She's been keeping an eye on shit for me."

Bull looked up at the chubby clerk with an old-style hairdo, who was smacking on gum. Bull cringed as he quickly finished securing her second leg and stood up.

"So, she's just gonna cover for us?" Bull asked as Connie turned her attention toward her tied up friend.

"Ty, who did this shit?" Connie asked.

"About three Mexican muthafuckas. They was short, and only one of them seemed to speak English. They threatened me to give them the security tape or they was gonna kill me," Tyronique responded as Connie smiled.

Connie showed Bull the tape as he shook his head.

"A fuckin' tape? Seriously. What kind of hotel still uses tapes?" Bull questioned.

"Stop your bitchin' and let's go," Connie said before she quickly grabbed the duct tape from her partner.

She quickly tore a piece off and placed it on her friend's mouth after she kissed her on the lips. Bull looked on with disgust.

"Thank you, baby girl. I'll hook you up a little

later," Connie said.

Tyronique nodded her head as Connie quickly picked a nearby desk phone and dialed 911.

"Hey! Oh my god, I think I heard gunshots at the Friendly Inn Hotel! Sounds like a bunch of Mexicans," Connie said in her best white girl dialect before she hung up the phone.

Connie looked toward Bull, who seemed impressed with her plan.

"Come on, nigga. No time for that shit. Let's go!" Connie said as she quickly made her way out of the lobby, followed closely by Bull.

The two jumped into Bull's vehicle, and he quickly started the engine before pulling off. Connie breathed a sigh of relief as she looked at the tape that they took from the hotel. She ripped the tape up and took another deep breath before relaxing, looking at Bull. He started laughing as the two partners both shared a laugh with each other while they continued down the road onto the highway.

Chapter 3

Revelations

Just a little after eleven at night, Club Exotica was packed as per usual with the dance floor, booths, and bar area all filled to capacity. The upstairs VIP just outside of Sharice's office was also packed and the building was filled with nightlife excitement.

Tucked away in her office, Sharice who was sitting next to Jerome in the nook area next to the window as they both shared a passionate kiss. Sharice backed away and giggled as Jerome chuckled himself.

"Look at you. All smiles and shit now," Jerome said. "You see, I was always the only one who could keep you smilin' like that. Shoulda never left me as far as I'm concerned."

"Yeah, whatever," a flip Sharice said as she rose and headed back to her desk.

Jerome laughed as he took a seat across from her.

"You know I'm right, but moving on, let's ditch this joint and go back to my place. Or yours. It doesn't matter," Jerome said.

"I got a meeting with the crew here in minute, Rome. I 'then told you that like six times now," Sharice said.

"So? You're the boss, remember? The crew meets when you say so. You need a break, a night of relaxation and shit," Jerome responded.

"Nigga, you just tryin' to get some ass, so kill all that relaxation shit you talkin'," Sharice quipped back.

Jerome got up from his chair and walked over next to Sharice before dropping down on one knee and grasping her hand.

"Yes, that is correct. I need the ass," Jerome joked.

"I mean, it's not like rainbows are shootin' out of your shit, but it is something I have a taste for that only you can provide, ya heard me."

Sharice shook her head as she gave her lover a look of disbelief.

"So, you sayin' my shit ain't magically delicious?" Sharice fired back. "'Cause, baby, I don't need rainbows shooting out my shit. I am the fuckin' rainbow, ya heard me?"

Jerome chuckled as he touched Sharice's exposed leg, and slowly began making his way up her skirt, between her thighs.

"Come on, baby. Let me have a taste of the rainbow if it's so magically delicious," Jerome pleaded.

Sharice smiled as she took his hand and removed it from her leg.

"Not now," she replied. "Let me handle my business, and I'll get with you later, okay?"

Jerome lowered his head in defeat, and the two

lovers were suddenly surprised by Michelle, who entered the office. She noticed Sharice sitting behind her desk, and was stunned to see Jerome's head rising from behind the desk.

"Oh shit! My bad. Guess I'm early. I'll... I'll come back," she said as she slowly backed away towards the door.

"No, Chelle, you're good. Jerome was just leaving," Sharice said, disappointing Jerome, who got off his knee.

"I guess I am," he said.

"Hey, don't go too far," Sharice instructed him. "We'll get you a box of Lucky Charms tonight. I'm tellin' you, you gonna love it."

Jerome chuckled as he kissed Sharice on the cheek.

"Aight, I'll be downstairs," he said before he made his way out of the office.

Michelle chuckled as she took a seat across from Sharice.

"Well, that seems to be going well," she said as Sharice straightened out her skirt.

"Yeah, it is," she responded with a hint of concern in her eyes. "That's what scares me."

"Scares you? Why?"

Sharice sighed as she went into her desk drawer and pulled out a couple of glasses and a bottle of vodka. She poured both her and Michelle a drink and took a quick sip before responding.

"Let me ask you this. This thing we're in, and what we do. Can you really maintain a relationship through this?" Sharice asked.

"Yeah, you can. I'm doing it now, but it's not easy," Michelle said, surprising her boss.

"You're in a relationship?"

"Yeah. Does that surprise you?" Michelle asked before she took a sip of her drink.

"Actually, it does," Sharice admitted. "You didn't mention that when we first sat down."

"Well, shit, I didn't know who I was fucking was

part of the interview process," Michelle quipped, causing Sharice to chuckle.

"So how long y'all been together?"

"A little over a year," Michelle answered.

"And he doesn't give you any shit being a part of this?" Sharice asked.

"Shit, the nigga don't even know I'm in the game," Michelle responded, confusing Sharice.

"Come again?"

"He don't know nothin' about this. Probably leave my ass if he knew," Michelle responded, still confusing Sharice.

"I'm not understanding. How in the fuck doesn't he know about this shit? I mean, he don't ask where you've been, or shit like that?" she asked.

"See, he would, if I didn't prep for it," Michelle answered. "Peep game, he thinks I'm a floating manager for Winn Dixie. Sometimes I have to work long hours, overnight stocking, shit like that. I have a store manager out in Metairie who covers for me if

Theo ever stops over. Tells him I'm working at another store or some shit, and hits me up to let me know he asked about me. Maybe about once a month, I work at the store and meet him there for lunch or whatever. If it was just some random nigga, I wouldn't trip, but I'm feelin' him, so it's worth it, I guess."

Sharice was amazed at the great lengths that Michelle was willing to go through to keep her business and love life separated. She quickly topped off Michelle's glass.

"Yeah. See, you need this more than I do," Sharice responded.

Michelle chuckled as she raised her drink and held it up for a toast. Sharice toasted her as they both took a sip of their drinks.

"Believe it or not, you got it easy, for real," Michelle said. "I mean, your dude knows what you're in, and he still down with you. No sneakin' or all the shit I gotta do. I envy you 'cause it's all easy. You don't have to leave your crib wearin' a Winn Dixie uniform every day."

Sharice looked at Michelle as she tried to imagine her wearing a Winn Dixie uniform. Michelle noticed her glare.

"What?"

"I'm just tryin' to picture you in a Winn Dixie uniform," Sharice joked.

"It's in the car. You wanna see it?" Michelle said.

Sharice laughed while she nodded her head, wanting to see Michelle in her fake job shirt.

"I might. I just might," she responded when James, Bull, and Connie entered into the office.

Connie frowned when she noticed Michelle and Sharice sharing a laugh.

"What's all this shit?" Connie inquired.

"Nothin', we just up here chillin' waitin' on all y'all to show up," Sharice answered.

"Well, some of us had to work before comin' in," Connie fired back as she looked towards Michelle.

"Well, some of us handle our business early, so we can play at night," Michelle quipped as Sharice ended the conversation.

"Enough of that shit, y'all two," Sharice said as she rose from her seat to come around her desk to address her crew. They all took a seat in the office.

"Look, I wanted to meet up because there's a threat going on in the streets," Sharice announced. "Found out this morning that some niggas on Sixth and Baronne have beef with us, and have attempted to take me and Connie out at least twice that we know of."

The crew all looked at each other with concern as Sharice calmed them down.

"Now, first things first, these ain't no big-time niggas. Just some corner boys who were very disrespectful to me and Connie once. They are led by Dre, a nigga I had to pop in his leg. My guess is he felt some type of way about that shit and is now comin' for me," Sharice explained.

"When all this shit happened?" asked James as Sharice turned her attention towards Bull.

"Well, that's the next thing we were gonna discuss because it involves you, Bull," she pointed out, shocking him.

"Me? What'd I do?"

"The night of the car jackin', me and Connie were supposed to meet you at the pool hall. Remember that?" Sharice asked Bull, who responded with a head nod. "Well, just before we arrived, there was a shootin'. Two women were shot dead, not even a block down from the hall."

"Okay. Tragic," Bull responded, not understanding what this had to do with him.

"Connie, did you get with Diego this morning like I told you?" Sharice asked.

"Yeah. He said them bitches wasn't connected to nobody. Just shot to shit for being in the wrong place at the wrong time," she responded as Sharice nodded her head.

Bull was still confused.

"Okay. I mean, you can get shot out here for half a dozen reasons," Bull responded.

"Not like that," Sharice interjected. "These women were executed. It wasn't a robbery or any shit like that. I just find it very coincidental that the same night me and Connie was supposed to be walkin' to the hall, two other women were gunned down in the same area. And you know how I am with coincidental shit."

Bull finally caught on what was being implied as anger filled his eyes.

"The fuck you tryin' to say, Sharice?" Bull said. "You sayin' I tried to have you wacked?! After all the shit I did for you?!"

"You're right. You have done so much for me," Sharice responded. "Anyone else... well, let's just say I wasn't totally convinced. However, I had Michelle let you know where me and Connie were going to be this morning, and guess what? Another squad of hittas was outside the beauty shop waitin'."

The room was silent as tension filled the air. Both Sharice and Bull stared down each other as the others become nervous.

"Was it money, Bull?" Sharice said. "Was it power? I treated you better than your own fuckin' kind, and this is the thanks I get?!"

"I did not do this shit, I swear on my mother," Bull said as he rose from his chair making Connie nervous as she gripped her gun behind her back.

"So, these niggas just randomly set up shop at the only fuckin' place that you knew about?" Sharice said. "Both times?! Come on, Bull! You think I'm gonna buy this shit?! You was the only one who knew where we were! At least do me the favor of not treatin' like some curb bitch! When did the nigga approach you?"

"What are you deaf?" Bull responded with anger filling his eyes. "I just fuckin' told you I don't know what you're talkin' about! I never heard of Dre, and I don't even know where the fuck Sixth and Barrone is!

I have never took a dime from anyone other than you, Sharice. I would never go against the crew with this shit!"

Sharice looked deep into Bull's eyes and can tell he was telling the truth. It still didn't make sense, since he was the only one who knew about their location both times. After a few moments, she backed down as she tried to figure things out.

"Did you mention this shit in passin'?" she asked.

"What?"

"Anything about us. Did someone ask you somethin' about us or any shit like that?"

"No. When you called me about the car jackin' shit, I was about to meet with the Asian guy that one time. It was just me and Ritchie in the car that day," Bull explained as Sharice and Connie looked at each other.

"What about yesterday? Where were you when Chelle called you?" Sharice asked.

"I was at my cousin's wedding," Bull responded as

Sharice approached him once more.

"Was Ritchie there with you too?" she asked.

"Yeah, he was sittin' at the table with me. I remember because he..."

Bull went silent as he came to the realization of what happened. His legs became weak as he quickly took a seat back into his chair.

"Because he what?" Sharice asked Bull.

"He... that son of a bitch... he overheard me talking to Michelle, and asked about where you get your hair done cause he was looking for a spot for his goomar," Bull said as Sharice breathed a sigh of relief.

She took a seat on top of her desk as the real enemy had been revealed.

"Let me guess, he overheard you talkin' to me the night of the car jackin' too?" Sharice asked.

Bull nodded his head as Sharice grabbed her head in frustration.

"How many times have I told y'all niggas to watch where you're takin' calls at?" Sharice said. "I mean, thank God it wasn't a fed or some shit like that. And Bull, you've been the game way too long to make that mistake."

Bull sighed as Sharice pondered her thoughts for a moment.

"So, what now?" Connie asked.

"What now?" Sharice said as she's offended. "You know what now. We have to nip it in the bud."

Bull looked up at Sharice and realized what she's saying. His friend had to go.

"Wait, hold on a minute," he replied. "This is a friend of mine. We came up together. We can't just wack him without anything more than that."

"Come on, Bull! You said it yourself; he was questionin' shit," Sharice reminded him. "Let me ask you this. How would y'all have handled this shit in y'alls thing back in the day? You tellin' me this shit would fly?"

Bull began to panic as his emotions took over. He knew what needed to be done, but couldn't kill one of his best friends over the allegations. He quickly stood up, and out of rage, tossed his chair to the other side of the room, making everyone around him nervous before he quickly made his way out of the office. Connie was about to go after him but was held back by Sharice.

"Let him go," she calmly said before she took her seat back behind her desk. "Alright, y'all all have reached out to the people on the corners and told them to change up, and watch their backs and shit, right?"

Everyone nodded as Sharice leaned back in her chair.

"Alright. Until we're able to handle this shit, y'all keep off the streets as best y'all can," Sharice instructed, which confused Connie.

"What the fuck are we waiting for?" Connie asked. "I can get some niggas together right now, run up on them, and be done before the sun comes up."

"Trust me, these niggas ain't doin' this shit by

themselves," Sharice responded. "They don't have them kinda balls to go at us like that. We need to see who else they down with. We already found one snitch in the crew. What if there are others? We need to plan this shit out."

Connie nodded her head with understanding as Sharice waved both James and Michelle out of the office. After they're both gone, Sharice turned her attention to Connie.

"What I say about being patient?" Sharice snapped. "I mean, you can't just run up on niggas all the time! Think Constance, damn!"

Connie sighed as she nodded her head with understanding once again.

"Did you get with the Columbian?" Sharice asked.

"Yeah, I took care of it."

"What did he say?"

Connie went silent for a moment as Sharice waited for a response.

"He didn't say anything," Connie said as she

fidgets.

"The fuck you mean, he didn't say anything?" Sharice asked.

"It means I took care of it, damn," Connie responded to a shocked Sharice.

"Connie, please tell me you didn't off this nigga?" Sharice said as Connie remained quiet.

An enraged Sharice came from behind her desk once again and approached her friend, who is looking on fearfully.

"What the fuck is wrong with you?!" Sharice exclaimed. "Do you know what you just did?! Do you know how the Columbians handle niggas who fuckin' kill one of theirs?! They light niggas on fire, Connie, then extinguish the flames just for fun. I told you how they handle folks, and you still went out there to kill this nigga? Are you outta your fuckin' mind?! It could be weeks before they give you the pleasure of dyin'. Does that sound like some shit you wanna go through?!"

Connie remained silent as Sharice grabbed her head in frustration.

"Look, I did what I had to do," Connie responded. "Reese, you know this nigga wasn't gonna let us slide with that bullshit. It couldn't be helped."

Sharice shook her head as she calmed down and took a seat next to her friend.

"Was it clean?" Sharice asked.

"Of course."

"No witnesses, or anything that can come back to fuck us," Sharice asked.

"No, I'm tellin' you, we kept it tight," Connie answered. "Even got the security tape from my homegirl that works there."

Sharice shot a look at Connie.

"Homegirl? What homegirl," she asked.

"You don't know her. Friend of mine from around the way," Connie answered. "She's tight, we made it look like some Hispanics did it. Left her tied up and shit, so when the cops arrive, they'll buy it. Trust me,

Reese, we're on it."

Sharice was silent, considering her options to make sure the issue is completely resolved. After a few moments, she rose from her seat and looked at her.

"Take care of your friend," Sharice said before she made her way back behind her desk to a shocked Connie.

"Reese, come on. We don't have to-"

"Connie, your plan was good, and it will clear us with the laws, but you think she's gonna hold up when the Columbians get their hands on her?" Sharice asked. "Trust me, you'll be doing her a favor compared to what they're gonna do to her. Make sure she disappears. I promise you, it's for the best. Or, leave her breathing and take your chances that she won't talk. It's on you."

Connie pondered her thoughts for a moment before agreeing to make the hit on her friend.

"I'll take care of it," Connie said. "I'm sure the

place is still crawling with cops, so I'll take care of it first thing tomorrow."

"Take care of it tonight," Sharice ordered. "And take Chelle with you."

"I don't need that bitch to handle this," Connie snapped back.

"Well, you and Bull have a history of makin' bad fuckin' decisions lately, and since he's not here anyway, you need back up. You go over there, wait for the police to clear out, and as soon as they do, make her disappear for all our sakes."

Sharice poured herself another small drink and downed it quickly before grabbing her purse and jacket. She looked a Connie once more before she made her way out of her office, leaving her emotional friend alone with her thoughts.

Later that night, Ritchie and a few other associates were having drinks and laughing in a local bar in midtown. It was a bar filled mostly with

Italians and was a typical set up with TVs, a jukebox, and finger foods. Ritchie was ordering another drink when Bull rushed into the bar and quickly located his friend. He made his way over to the bar area and approached him.

"Ritchie, I need to talk to you," Bull said.

"Hey, Bull, my friend, pull up a stool. We're just talking about how back in Jersey we would-"

"Ritchie, I need to talk to you now," a serious Bull said, interrupting his friend.

Ritchie noticed the look on Bull's face and nodded his head before turning to the bartender.

"Hey, Tony, watch my seat. I'll be back," he said as he followed Bull outside of the bar.

As soon as they're outside of the bar, Bull looked around before he addressed his friend.

"Did you set up Sharice to get whacked?" Bull bluntly asked, which caught Ritchie off guard.

"Excuse me?"

"Did you set up our boss to get whacked?"

Ritchie chuckled and shook his head in disbelief.

"Well, a lot a good it did. I heard she was still breathin' unless you're here to tell me different," he responded, enraging Bull, who grabbed him by his jacket, pinning him to the wall of the building.

"You son of a bitch! What did you do?" Bull asked as Ritchie struggled to get loose. "Why would you do that, huh? Why the fuck would you pull a move like that?"

"Because you don't have the balls to do it yourself," Ritchie fired back. "I mean, in all seriousness, taking orders from a ditsoon, and a fuckin' broad at that? Come on! It was only a matter of time before someone took her out."

"Oh, so you trade working for her to another ditsoon?" Bull responded. "Yeah, that makes a lot of sense!"

"Who the fuck are you kiddin'?" Ritchie replied. "You told me back in the day she was a pain in the balls. They offered me money, and position in the new organization, but make no mistake about it, it's only temporary. This mulignan ain't the brightest. Eventually, I'll take over and have my own thing working."

"Sharice is smarter than you think," Bull replied. "She knows you tried to have her whacked!"

"Oh, I see. She sent you here to take me out," Ritchie questioned. "Well, go ahead then. Side with the bitch, and do what you came here for!"

Bull grit his teeth because he knew what he had to do, but hesitated as his emotions overtake his thoughts. He slowly backed away from his friend as he released his hold on him. Ritchie smiled as he straightened himself out before he approached his friend.

"Look, I know you gotta thing for the broad, but she's not one of us. I knew you wouldn't go for it, so I took it off you and put it on me," he said to a conflicted Bull.

"But... there's rules to this thing," Bull replied.

"What thing? Their thing? Come on, the niggers and spics never go by the rules," Ritchie responded. "I mean, even our thing ain't what it once was from what I hear back home. We got captains getting' whacked in front of McDonalds back in Jersey over a comment made to someone's daughter. The old times, they're gone. It's why Johnny Boy left when he did. He saw this shit as an opportunity. Now, look at him, Faction Boss. Once we stabilize shit down here, you think he's not gonna wanna deal with his own kind? Get outta here."

A silent Bull pondered his next move.

"What do you mean, once 'we' stabilize shit?" Bull asked.

Ritchie walked up to his friend, placed his hands on Bull's shoulder, and looked him square in his eyes.

"You think I'd forget you in all this?" Ritchie said. "This is the thing me and you were made for. If I go up, you go up. Now, I'm not gonna ask you to take care of the broad. I know that's too much. My guy will take care of that. Once it's over though, I expect you to man up and help me take back these streets. I'd give it less than a year. The shine will be out and we'll be on top. What do ya say?"

Bull stood speechless and confused as Ritchie looked at him, knowing he was conflicted.

"Tell you what, you think on it," Ritchie said as he tapped him on his cheek. "Either way, it's gonna get done. Either you're with us, or you're against us. I promise you, Bull. You don't wanna be on the other end of this thing."

Ritchie took one last look at his friend before he made his way back into the bar. Bull was beside himself with this new revelation. He stared blankly into space as he considered his options for several moments before he made his way toward his car.

A few hours later, Connie noticed the last police car pull out of the hotel where she and Bull killed the Columbian earlier that night from her car parked down the block. She started her car, pulled into the parking lot, and cautiously looked around. She pulled out her cell phone, texted Tyronique, and waited for her to arrive outside.

Several moments later, Tyronique made her way out of the hotel lobby, smiling. She waved at Connie as she quickly got into the passenger's side of the vehicle.

"Hey, girl. Didn't know you were rollin' back through?" she said.

"Yeah, I was in the area and noticed the cops had all left. How'd that shit go?" Connie asked.

"Just like you said. They got a APB out on some Spanish niggas that don't exist. Told them I feared for my life and shit. It's all good, I held it down," Tyronique replied much to Connie's satisfaction.

"That's good to hear. I got your money," Connie said as she reached in her pocket.

She never handed her friend the cash-filled envelope. Michelle rose up from the back seat and quickly wrapped a wire around Tyronique's neck, choking her. Connie did her best to hold her friend down, which allowed Michelle to cut off their victim's windpipe. After a few minutes of struggling, Tyronique's body finally went limp as her life faded. Connie checked her out before waving Michelle off.

Michelle released her grip as Connie looked at her dead friend with regret.

"I didn't know the bitch was that big," Michelle said as Connie shot her a frown.

"Don't ever disrespect her like that again," Connie fired back. "She was a friend of mine."

Michelle rolled her eyes as she sat back in her seat.

"Whatever. Seems like you ain't shit as a friend," Michelle quipped as Connie received a text. She quickly checked it out and smiled before turning her attention to Michelle.

"Aye, look, I gotta go take care of something. Make sure she disappears, ya head me?" Connie said as she opened the car door.

A confused Michelle quickly jumped out of the car and cut Connie off.

"Wait, what?" she said. "You want me to do this shit by myself?"

"Yeah, Reese needs me to take care of some shit. High level," Connie responded. "Not a trace."

Michelle was still confused as she watched Connie walk off. After several moments, Michelle shook her head in disgust as she got back into the car on the driver's side. She looked at Tyronique's dead body and became more enraged.

"What the fuck is your fat ass you lookin' at?" Michelle said as she pushed the body to the side and started the car.

She quickly pulled off and headed down the road, hoping and praying she didn't get stopped by the police.

It's almost dawn, as Davis was at one of the

monitoring stations in the FBI safe house amazed while he watched a live streaming video of Rose and Connie having sex in the apartment the feds set up for her. Daniels walked in with a couple of coffees in his hand. He handed one to Davis before he took a seat next to his partner.

"Are they still at it?" he questioned before he sipped his coffee.

"Yes, can you believe that?" Davis responded. "I haven't had this good of sex since college, and even then, I'm not sure. I mean, this is like watching internet porn."

Daniels chuckled as she took a look at the monitor.

"These new cameras are stunning," he said. "Is the audio good?"

"See for yourself," Davis said as he removed the earphones from the jack to reveal a lot of moaning and grunting between the two women.

Daniels waved his partner off as Davis put the

headphones back in the jack.

"Well, I have good news. I got approval for the lighter bug. They're gonna airship it to us by tomorrow. So, we should be able to make the change tonight, unless Connie becomes tired of her," Daniels said.

Davis looked at the monitor and observed the two women who continued to have a passionate sex session.

"Yeah, I think we're good on that front," Davis joked as Daniels looked at several files that were piled up on the desk next to him.

Davis looked on with concern and turned his attention towards his partner.

"Look, Daniels, I hate to keep bringing this up, but are we seriously going to allow this to keep going on?" Davis asked. "I mean, I know it's happened before where undercover agents had to do what they do, but this seems a little different."

Daniels nodded his head with agreement.

"I agree. That's why once she swaps out the lighter and returns the gun, we're pulling her out. We should have what we need by then, and there's no reason for us to continue putting her at risk," he replied. "According to informant 6840, Sharice is in the middle of a war. I don't want Flores caught up in the middle of that. Sooner we can make the switch, the better."

Davis nodded his head before turning his attention back to the monitor.

About an hour had gone by and Connie had finally went to sleep. Rose looked around before looking into the camera, and signaled that she's about to swap out the gun. Daniels, who was watching the monitor, snapped his fingers to wake up his partner.

"She's about to make the switch," Daniels said as Davis quickly made his way over to the monitor to observe the operation.

Rose quietly exited the bed, reached between the mattress, and pulled out the replica gun. She then tiptoed softly to the other side of the bed and located her mark's gun. She made one last quick comparison before she made the swap. Once again, she was able to complete the operation without detection. She placed the real gun between the mattress where the dummy gun was initially located and quickly hopped back in bed without alerting Connie. She threw a thumbs up to the camera, much to the relief of both Daniels and Davis.

"Well, one down, one to go," Davis said.

Daniels nodded his head in agreement before he took a deep breath, relieved that everything went according to plan.

Chapter 4

Fuck Friends

As the sun began to set in the city, a slight breeze filled the air. Jerome's car pulled up on the nearby curb of a pretty run-down neighborhood. He looked around in confusion as he turned to Sharice, who was on the passenger's side of the car.

"This is where you're meetin' someone?" he asked. "Shit, you might get robbed tryin' to meet up with someone out here."

Sharice went into her purse and revealed her gun, which put Jerome's thoughts at ease.

"I'm good," she said.

"I can see that."

The couple sat quietly for a moment, as they enjoyed each other's presence for a little while longer.

"You sure you can't just blow this shit off?" Jerome said. "You could always meet up with whoever another day, ya heard me?"

Sharice chuckled before she responded.

"You just want some more ass," she quipped back. "You ain't slick."

Jerome laughed as he nodded his head.

"I ain't gonna lie, you got me hooked, baby," he responded. "But to be real, I'm just enjoyin' myself with you lately. This could have been us a long time ago, but you were actin' funny."

"I'll admit, I could have done shit differently, you know," Sharice responded. "Fact is we're here now. Whatever happened way back when doesn't matter."

Jerome nodded his head, as he and Sharice shared one final kiss. Sharice smiled as she opened the car door.

"You sure you don't need me to hang around?" Jerome asked.

"I'm good," Sharice responded. "Just keep this body on your mind, and you'll be fine."

A smirk entered Jerome's face as Sharice got out of the car and headed down the sidewalk. Jerome stuck around until Sharice faded from his view, entering a nearby apartment complex before he started his car and pulled off.

Back at the FBI monitoring station, Agent Flores, under her Rose guise, was meeting with both Agents Daniels and Davis. She handed them the gun she secured the night prior, which they took and bagged up for evidence.

"Good work, Flores," Daniels said as he tagged the gun. "I'll get this over to the lab boys, and see if there's anything on file. We also received authorization on the lighter too, and received the copy earlier today."

Davis handed the lighter to Flores, who inspected it thoroughly.

"Damn, that was fast. How'd you get them to process it so quick?" Flores asked.

"Once we laid out the plan, and got the judge to sign off, the bosses were all on board," Daniels responded. "How soon can you make the swap?"

"Well, she said she had something to do tonight, but I think I can persuade her to come on by after she's done," Flores said with a smile on her face.

"I bet you can," Davis joked.

Daniels nodded his head before continuing.

"That's good. As soon as the swap is made, we're pulling you out," he said to a stunned Flores.

"Pulling me out?" she questioned. "Why?"

"Sharice and her crew are in a war, according to our informants. We don't want you to get caught up in it. The bug gets us in on the inside, so there's no reason to risk your life unnecessarily," Daniels responded much to Flores' displeasure. "You did good work, but it's time to let the tech do its job."

"Come on, Daniels, we both know we need eyes on what's going on. Human eyes. Yeah, the tech can do its job, but the tech can't make judgment calls, or anything outside of what it was created for. You still need inside information, and I've made it in this far," Flores plead. "Daniels, you can't pull me out."

"Sorry, the decision has already been made," Daniels responded. "Get the bug in as quickly as you can, and you're done. Try and see if you can get her back to your apartment again so we can monitor the switch, but after that, we're clearing out anyone in harm's way."

Flores sighed as she shook her head in disagreement. Eventually, she pulled out her phone and texted Connie attempting to set up a meet.

Connie pulled up outside of an apartment complex when she received Flores, rather Rose's, text. A smile entered her face as she texted back that she would roll thru when she could. She looked around at the area and pulled out the card Diego gave her with the address of the witness. She exited the vehicle and made her way into the complex.

As she made her way through, she noticed several fiends in the complex walking around. She had a tight grip on her gun, which was concealed in her backstrap, as she made her way through the dangerous complex. She finally located the apartment she was looking for and noticed a light is on through the window. She looked around the area once more before she backed away and headed back down to her car.

She positioned her car where she could monitor the second-floor apartment window and continued to observe the area as she lit up a blunt to pass the time.

A couple of hours later, Connie was surfing the internet on her phone when she noticed the light going out in the apartment from her car. She waited a few more minutes before she exited the vehicle and made her way back through the complex as before. She arrived at the second-floor apartment door and placed her ear on the door as she tried to detect any sound for a few moments. After confirming there's no sound, she quickly put on a pair of gloves and went into her pocket to pull out a lock pick. She quickly picked the lock and slowly opened the door, being careful not to make any noise.

As she tiptoed into the apartment and quietly closed the door behind her, she slowly kicked off her shoes, pulled her gun out, and slowly made her way deeper into the apartment. Beads of sweat began to fill her head as she checked every corner of the apartment to ensure she didn't miss anything. The first door she passed was a bathroom door. She took a quick peek inside before she moved on. She looked towards the only bedroom door in the apartment.

She took her time as she slowly opened the bedroom door and made her way in. She was caught off guard as the light suddenly came on, revealing Sharice, who was sitting on the bed with anger-filled eyes. Connie was stunned when she noticed her friend in the apartment.

"Sharice? I... I..." Connie said in an attempt to form words.

Sharice rose to her feet and walked up to Connie, who still had her gun drawn.

"I was hopin' it wasn't you," Sharice said with a frown. "Anybody but you! I fuckin' knew it! I really did, but seeing you here now really breaks my fuckin' heart!"

A nervous Connie finally lowered her weapon, still speechless as Sharice waited for an explanation.

"Say something, bitch!" Sharice yelled. "Explain to me why you would hurt me like this! Why the fuck would you rip my heart out?! Why would you kill our friend?!"

"Sharice, I... I... look, it's not what you think. I was-"

Sharice slapped Connie in the face, sending her down to her knees before she pulled out her gun and pointed it at Connie's head. A distraught Connie dropped her gun and looked to her friend for mercy.

"Please, Sharice. Please don't do this," she begged her friend.

"You got the nerve to ask for mercy? Are you fuckin' kiddin' me?" Sharice replied. "Why, Connie? Why would you break my fuckin' heart! Why!"

An emotional Sharice had a few tears that flowed down her face as Connie's emotions got the best of her as well.

"Break your heart? You broke mine first," Connie fired back. "I fuckin' love you! You know that! I would do anything for you, and for you to do what you did!"

"What did I do?" Sharice questioned. "What did I do that was so hurtful that you would kill our friend?!"

"You gave yourself to her!" Connie shouted,

releasing all the pinned up anger she had been carrying. "You talked all that shit about not being down and shit, and you only like niggas, but then you end up in that bitch's bed? Are you fuckin' kidding me?"

"I told you about that after you killed her, so that's bullshit," Sharice responded.

"Nah, I was there! I was there outside the door when you and her had y'all's little discussion," Connie revealed. "I heard the whole fuckin' thing. That bitch took one of my girls once, and then she took you from me. Anyone but me! It's like Jerome comes back in your life, and you run with him and shit. I wouldn't be surprised if Tracy fucked you at this point. Just anyone but me, the one who loves you the most!"

The anger in Sharice's eyes continued to build as she held onto her gun firmly pointed as Connie's head.

"Number one, I don't belong to you! Who and

how many people I fuck ain't got shit to do with you," Sharice fussed. "Second, I told you it was a mistake. I didn't go there to fuck Lavina. I even told her if she flirts with me again, I was done with her. That shit that happened doesn't change what I am. Even if it did, your beef shoulda been with me, not her! You killed her, Connie. You fuckin' killed her!"

Sharice cocked back the hammer of her gun as Connie braced for the shot.

"Vina's sister told me when I found out who killed her to make them pay. She told me to make them suffer, and I gave her my word I would," Sharice told Connie. "Give me one fuckin' reason why I shouldn't carry that out."

Connie had no reason why Sharice should spare her as tears began to flow down her face as well. After several moments, she looked up to Sharice from her knees and noticed the hurt in her eyes.

"Reese, I love you, and you know that," Connie replied. "Unlike the rest of these niggas in the game,

131

you know I do. I would never look to hurt you. You want the truth, well here it is. I went to confront Lavina about the shit, and we got into an argument. She attacked me, and I-"

"Bullshit! Bullshit!" Sharice interrupted. "Lavina would have never did some shit like that."

"I swear, Sharice. On my life, she did," Connie said. "She came at me, and we went back and forth for a min before I took it too far. I didn't go there for that, it just got outta hand."

"You see, that's your fuckin' problem, Connie! Shit always gets 'outta hand' with you," Sharice responded. "With this Columbian thing, the card game, and now this? Shit always gets outta hand, and I end up payin' the price for your bullshit! Because of you, my goddaughter doesn't have a mother, all over pussy you thought was yours!"

Connie closed her eyes as she felt Sharice had made her decision. She waited for the bullet as Sharice took a deep breath. The shot never came, however, because Sharice un-cocked her gun. Connie slowly opened her eyes as she looked towards her old friend.

"Killin' you is too easy. Besides, I'm sure the Columbians will catch up with your ass sooner or later," Sharice said. "I want you to live with the fact that you will never have me. In fact, me and you are done. You are no longer my number one. You report to Bull now, and thirty percent of everything you earn goes to Lavina's daughter. You are not to have access to my office or me unless I call for your ass. In fact, I don't want you even in the club. Seeing your face is always gonna remind me what you took from me."

A devastated Connie cried as Sharice put her gun away.

"Now get your shoes on and get the fuck outta here," Sharice ordered.

Connie struggled to get back to her feet as she wiped her face.

"Sharice, please can we-"

"Get the fuck outta here before I change my mind!" Sharice yelled as she shunned her friend.

A distraught Connie slowly made her way out of the bedroom and out of the apartment, leaving Sharice alone with her thoughts. After several moments, Sharice burst into tears crying uncontrollably. Sharice had lost two of her closest friends within a span of a couple of weeks, and the stress was too much for her to hold inside. She collapsed on the ground, left with only her grief and pain flowing through her.

The next morning, Sharice walked into her club, a little tipsy from several drinks she'd been drinking earlier that morning. She noticed Tracy sitting at a nearby table, going over paperwork.

"Hey, what you doing here?" Sharice said as she approached her friend.

"Hey, girl. Just going over some of these receipts

and orders," Tracy responded when she noticed Sharice's condition. "Looks like you have a rough night."

"You could say that," Sharice said as she took a seat across from Tracy.

"Lot of that going around. Bull is at the end of the bar down there gettin' wasted," she responded, causing Sharice to look towards the bar area before she turned her attention back to Tracy.

"So, you came in early just to do this?" she inquired.

"Nah, I actually pulled a Sharice and slept in your office after closing. Didn't make no sense going home," Tracy answered as she looked over a few receipts.

"Tracy, I'm starting to think you live here," Sharice joked. "I mean, damn girl, you're married with kids? How does that shit work out?"

"Well, hubby is out of town on business, and the kids are at my mom's house for the weekend. I don't

135

have a life outside of them, so I figured I might as well get some work done," Tracy explained.

Sharice nodded her head with understanding and was about to get up when she turned back to her friend.

"Hey, just an FYI, me and Connie had a fallin' out. I don't want her anywhere near me no more," Sharice said, shocking her friend. "No access to my office at all. I banned her from the club too, but she's gonna be workin' with Bull, so that may be a little unreasonable, but don't give her access to my office anymore."

"Hold up. What happened, Reese?" Tracy asked.

Sharice was about to confess everything to her friend but decided against it at the last minute.

"Let's just say I don't trust her anymore," Sharice responded.

"Reese, we just lost Lavina. How you gonna lose another friend while she's still here?" Tracy asked. "I mean, it can't be that bad, can it?"

Sharice chuckled as she rose from her chair.

"Just don't give her office access, okay?" she said before abruptly walking off toward the bar area.

She noticed Bull was drinking some whiskey and was a little tipsy himself. She took a seat next to him, not saying a word, and grabbed a nearby glass. Bull noticed her and poured her a drink. Sharice took a big gulp and downed her drink quickly as she waved to Bull to pour her another one.

"What's got you so drunk this morning?" Bull said as he poured her another drink.

"The same thing that got you fucked up," Sharice replied. "Fuckin' friends."

Bull was confused as he took a sip of his drink.

"I know you're pretty gone right now, but I'm gonna tell you anyway. Connie now reports to you. I don't want anything else to do with her ass. How ever y'all work that shit out is up to you," Sharice shared with a surprised Bull.

Sharice noticed his glare as she continued to sip

on her drink.

"Yeah, nigga. You ain't the only one with friend issues. Did you take care of it?" she asked.

Bull shook his head.

"I couldn't do it," he responded.

"Yeah, I know the feelin'," Sharice said. "Just hold off. I'll get someone else on it. It was wrong for me to put it on you in the first place."

Bull nodded his head as he chuckled a bit.

"You know, me and Ritchie came over together. Here I was, a punk kid tryin' to get on with the Moretti family out in Jersey. Just being a Made Man was somethin' I dreamed of. Ritchie told me that Johnny Boy was down south makin' waves, and we need to run with him," Bull said. "I didn't wanna do it, but Ritchie was my guy, and he said there was more opportunity with John than with the Moretti family. So I said, fuck it, let's go. We came down here and joined John, later settled on New Orleans, and the rest is history."

Sharice nodded her head surprised Bull was opening up to her like he hadn't before.

"Well, seems like you made the right call," Sharice replied.

"More than you know," Bull responded. "A few years after we left, there was a war between the Moretti family and the DeCavalcante family. Needless to say, the entire Moretti family was wiped out. I wasn't made, so maybe that doesn't happen to me, or maybe it does. Who knows? Ritchie, he knew though. He knew that there was no future with the Moretti crew. I couldn't see it. He's always one step ahead."

Sharice ponder for a few moments as she began to chuckle herself.

"I don't know why, but you just reminded me of how me and Connie met," Sharice said. "Here I am, on Canal street gettin' jumped by these three Fortier bitches 'cause I went to a school they were beefin' with. I wasn't into all that shit, but they kept pressin' me, so I punched one bitch, and the other two jumped in. I am gettin' my ass beat when out of nowhere, Connie jumps in and starts whippin' on them bitches."

Bull smiled as Sharice managed a smirk too.

"She didn't even know me, but she looked out for me, and we ran them hoes off. Said us Kennedy hoes gotta stick together. After that, we became cool and shit. She was always in the drug game, tryin' to hustle and shit. Me, I was still tryin' to find my purpose. She brought me in, showed me the ropes. I don't know, maybe I did move up too fast and left her behind, but I told her that fuckin' temper, that... that shit that makes her so good for the corner is also what makes her so bad for everything else. Still... she was there for me when nobody else was. Breaks my fuckin' heart."

Bull continued to look on confused as Sharice finished her second drink.

"Reese, are you okay?" Bull asked.

"No Bull, I'm not," Sharice replied. "But like all

things, time will heal all."

"So, who's gonna be your number one now?" Bull asked.

Sharice shrugged while she looked at him.

"Why? You want the job?" Sharice asked.

Bull chuckled at the notion.

"Spendin' my day driving you to the beauty and nail shop and sittin' in the car while you do God knows what? Forget about it," Bull responded, causing Sharice to smirk.

"Yeah. I figured. Guess I'll bring Michelle along. She seems motivated," Sharice responded before she raised her empty glass. "To friends?"

Bull toasted Sharice and downed his drink.

"To friends," he repeated.

"Yeah, fuck 'em," Sharice said as she struggled to maintain her balance initially before she regained her composure.

She slowly made her way upstairs to her office and took a seat behind her desk. She removed her heels before kicking her feet on top of her desk. She leaned back in her chair, trying to finally get some rest after the past day's events.

The waves from the lake rippled as the breeze in the area moved them along their projected path. The sun beamed brightly as it began to set lighting the area up with its reddish-yellow glow. On the lakefront area, at a nearby picnic table overlooking the lakefront, J Rock, Danky, Ritchie, and others were waiting for the arrival Dre, who finally pulled into the parking lot with Lil Dee driving. Both of them exited the vehicle and made their way toward the meeting area. Dre was moving a lot faster but still has to use a cane to get around. He took a seat at the table as the meeting commences.

"Bad news," Ritchie said. "She knows it's you tryin' to hit her. If you're gonna make a move, now's the time."

"Dee has some info on that," Dre responded as he

turned his attention towards his cousin.

"Yeah, check it out. We gotta guy who can make the hit," Lil Dee announced. "Thing is, this nigga wants twenty-five large to do the job. Fifteen upfront, the rest when it's done."

Danky, J Rock, and Ritchie all were surprised by the quote as they discussed it with each other.

"That's a bit steep, don't you think?" J Rock replied. "I remember when you could get niggas hit for under five g's."

"Yeah well, this nigga ain't dumb. He knows who she is, and who she's connected with," Lil Dee responded. "He also knows about the Feds being posted up outside of the club too. This ain't no easy fuckin' job. If y'all don't wanna break that bread, then y'all niggas are gonna need to figure out a new plan then. He's the only hitta that would take the job."

The group was silent as they considered their options when Dre chimed in.

"Look, if y'all want me to front the green for this

shit, then fuck it, I'll do it," Dre said. "But keep in mind, K-One shit, and some of them Faction corners are gonna come to me if I do. We agreed at the beginning of this thing that we was all gonna share this shit. That includes the risks involved. You niggas can't just be here for the good shit. If I gotta shoulder this shit, then I'm gonna do it at a price."

J Rock and Danky looked at each other and nodded before responding.

"Aight, I'm in," Danky declared. "Whatever we need to do to end this shit."

"Me too," J Rock said. "When is this shit gonna go down?"

"The sooner, the better," Dre said as he turned his attention back toward his cousin. "When can he do that shit?"

"As soon as he gets the fifteen, he said he can knock it out within seventy-two hours," Lil Dee responded. "If y'all want that nigga to move, then get the money to us asap."

J Rock and Danky agreed as they all dapped Dre before making their way off, leaving Ritchie, Dre, and Lil Dee alone. Ritchie took a seat next to Dre as the two pondered what's next.

"So, the bitch knows about me?" Dre confirmed, causing Ritchie to nod his head.

"Yeah, guess she put two and two together. That means she's gonna be coming for you," Ritchie said.

"Man, fuck that bitch," Dre responded nonchalantly. "Let her ass come. I'll save us all the twenty-five and do that shit myself."

"Are you outta your fuckin' mind?" Ritchie asked. "Sharice is not a person who's gonna hit the streets. She has people for that!"

"Well, she hit the streets when she shot Dre in the leg," Lil Dee responded causing Dre to frown.

"Fuck all that. What is it that you want?" Dre asked Ritchie.

"I want you to take some time off. At least until the job is done," he responded. "You don't need to be on the corner exposin' yourself. Lay back until this thing winds down."

Dre considered his options for a moment before agreeing to Ritchie's request.

"Aight, I can do that," he said.

"Good. Anywhere you can rest your head for the next few days?"

"Yeah, I gotta spot," Dre said before he turned his attention to Lil Dee.

"Aye, make sure them niggas stay on point. I don't wanna come back after this shit is done hearin' excuses on why my money ain't right."

"I got you, no problem," Lil Dee responded as Dre rose to his feet.

"What about your man? You get anything that can help us out from him?" Dre asked Ritchie.

"Nah, nothing. Make sure your guy knows Bull isn't to be touched. He's a friend of mine. He'll come around once he removes his nose from her cunt," Ritchie said. "Make sure he knows who the targets are, and who the targets aren't. Wouldn't want another pool hall incident to fuck everything up again, now would we? I couldn't serve her up any better than I did that night."

"That shit was on me, I'll take that," Lil Dee admitted.

"Well, make sure you get it right this time," Ritchie said as he rose from his seat as well.

He nodded at Dre before making his way off, leaving Dre and Lil Dee alone.

"That nigga sure soundin' all boss like," Lil Dee said.

"Fuck that wop," Dre responded. "He's just a means to an end. Once he loses his worth, I'll smoke his spaghetti eatin' ass myself."

Lil Dee nodded his head as he and Dre made their way back to their car.

Chapter 5

Regrets

Agent Flores, in her guise as Rose, walked into the FBI monitoring base with a frown on her face she tossed the lighter on a nearby table where Davis and Daniels were sitting, which surprised both agents.

"Well, that was a fuckin' waste," she said as she took a seat, holding her head in frustration.

"What happened?" asked Daniels.

"Apparently, Connie and Sharice had a falling out," Flores responded. "She's been demoted. Sharice won't even let her in the damn office. The whole operation was a waste of fucking time!"

Daniels nodded his head as he picked up the

lighter Flores had tossed onto the table and placed it in an evidence bag.

"Well, here's some more bad news, the ballistics came back from the gun you lifted from Connie. The gun came back clean," he said, which furthered Flores' frustration.

"Son of a bitch. So all we have is a gun charge on the girl?" Flores replied. "She's not gonna flip on that bullshit ass charge! All this work for nothing!"

Daniels pondered for several moments as he noticed Flores' frustration.

"I'm going to make a judgment call. I'm going to allow you to maintain your undercover status," Daniels said, which surprised Flores.

"Really?"

"Like you said, the operation is a bust. All we have is a weapon's charge and still are no closer to Sharice, with them falling out with each other. We still need eyes on the inside, and somebody to continue to work the crew," Daniels explained to a grateful

Flores. "I will, however, pull you if things get too hot. We know a war is brewing between her and a local crew, and I won't hesitate to pull you if I need to."

Flores nodded her head in agreement, happy to continue her undercover operation. After a few moments, Flores' mind wandered into an idea.

"Not for nothing, but has anyone tried to approach Sharice?" Flores said. "I mean, someone just going up to her and telling her that her life is in danger. I know it's a long shot, but at least we can sit down with her and feel her out. Just a thought."

Daniels and Davis both looked at each other as Davis nodded his head. Daniels was a little reluctant.

"I mean, aren't you the least bit curious about her?" he asked his partner. "You've been monitoring her for months. Wouldn't it be nice to just have a quick chat with the girl? Worst case is we get a little more lay of the land of sorts, and maybe we can make her slip up. What's it going to hurt at this point?"

Daniels sighed as he looked at both Davis and

Flores. He went into his drawer and pulled out his gun, which is nestled into a holster.

"Let the surveillance team know we're on the way. We'll stake out the club until she arrives," Daniels said as Davis quickly pulled out his phone to make the call.

Daniels turned his attention to Flores, who is a bit relieved with what's going on.

"So, why did Connie and Sharice fall out?" Daniels asked.

"Not sure. Connie was damn near in tears all last night. She kept mentioning something about their friend Lavina, but she wouldn't say anything beyond that," Flores responded as Lavina's name piqued Daniels interest.

He got up, walked over to a stack of files, and searched through them until he located the specific file he was looking for.

"That wouldn't happen to be Lavina James, would it?" Daniels asked.

"I didn't get a last name, but I mean, how many Lavina's could there be?" Flores said as she made her way over by Daniels.

He handed her a folder which had photos of Lavina, and several documents based on surveillance.

"Said here she's not in the game. Been out for a few years," Flores said.

"I know. What the file doesn't say since it hasn't been updated is Lavina was killed a little over a week ago at her massage parlor," Daniels said to a shocked Flores. "Apparently, the local police are calling it a burglary. She was strangled to death."

A blown away Flores was silent while she continued to read the file.

"You think Connie had something to do with it?" Flores asked.

"Not sure, but if she did, this would be reason for them to have beef," Daniels surmised. "Lavina and Sharice were childhood friends. She was in the game with her for a year or two but dropped off our radar about seven years ago after going legit. We never had anything on her, or even heard about her recently until this incident."

Daniels turned his attention toward Davis, who was getting ready to leave as well.

"Davis, get local on the phone. Have them fax over everything they have on the Lavina case," Daniels said before he stopped in his tracks. "You know what? Scratch that. We'll make a stop at the precinct on our way out to the club. We'll see if we can wrap this into our case."

Davis nodded his head as Daniels turned his attention back to Flores.

"Stay safe out there. Remember, the case isn't worth your life. Make the right calls," he said to Flores.

"I will, thanks," she responded before Daniels and Davis exited the office.

Flores continued to look over the paperwork on Lavina, studying every detail she could about

Sharice's longtime friend.

Sharice was sitting in her office not looking herself as Michelle sat across from her going over several details about their operation. Sharice was distant, thinking about the utter betrayal by Connie as their altercation constantly repeated in her head. All she heard were faint words until Michelle questioned her.

"Sharice?" Michelle said, causing Sharice to snap out of her thoughts.

"Yeah."

"Are you hearin' me?" Michelle asked.

"Yeah, I'm just... my bad, Chelle. I'm just not in the mood for this shit right now," Sharice said as she grabbed her head in frustration.

"Well, I'd probably be for it if I'm tryin' to cap a nigga before he caps me," Michelle warned. "Reese, he's gone underground. Ain't nobody seen him in a couple of days, which means he's about to strike first!

We need to plan for that."

Sharice took a deep breath before nodding her head.

"Fine. Make sure everyone knows the game plan. Make sure they watch their backs in the streets. We still need to find this nigga as quickly as we can. Get on the phone with Diego. He's supposed to been tracking this shit down for me. Also, get Bull on the phone and tell him I wanna get with him tonight. I know he doesn't wanna hear it, but his boy gonna have to go. We need to work him over if need be, which I know he's not gonna be for. He's the only one that can get close though," Sharice said.

Michelle nodded and was about to take out her cell phone when they are suddenly interrupted by a knock on the door. Tracy peeked in as Sharice waved her in.

"Hey, Trace. What's up?"

"Hey... umm... there's two FBI agents downstairs asking for you," Tracy said, causing Michelle to tense up.

"Do they have a warrant?" Sharice asked.

"Well... they say they're not here for that," Tracy answered. "They just said they wanna have a conversation with you."

Sharice turned to Michelle, both of them wearing looks of confusion.

"A conversation?"

"Yeah, that's what they're saying. Should I tell them to leave?"

Sharice pondered for a few seconds before shaking her head.

"Nah, send them up," Sharice said as Tracy made her way downstairs.

A panicked Michelle rose from her chair and approached Sharice, who was sitting behind her desk.

"What the fuck, Sharice?" Michelle said. "What are we gonna do?"

"How about calm the fuck down," Sharice fired back. "Trust me, if they were here for anything over a parkin' ticket, they wouldn't have asked. So chill the fuck out."

Michelle nodded her head as Tracy re-entered the office with Daniels and Davis behind her.

"Agents Daniels and Davis here to see you," Tracy announced before she backed out of the room.

Sharice waved them in as they approached her desk.

"Ms. Legget, my name is Agent Daniels," Daniels said. "May I have a seat?"

"No," Sharice said, catching the agents off guard. "So, if you don't have a warrant, why are you here? Fishin' for information, I assume? Or are you trying to have your Heat moment where I'm Robert Di Nero, and you're Al Pacino?"

Daniels chuckled as nodded his head.

"I love your taste in movies," he responded, getting a slick grin from Sharice. "No, actually I'm here because your life is in danger, and felt it was my duty to make you aware of that."

"Is that so?"

"I know you're no stranger to danger with what your line of business brings, but I'm hearing through my contacts that you may be panicking for the first time," Daniels said with a sly grin. "The Empress of New Orleans being shaken is news to us, so we'd thought we'd stop by and see if we can offer you a way out."

"A way out?" Sharice said as she looked at Michelle. "You hear that? They gonna offer me a way out."

Michelle nodded her head, acting as though she was impressed as Sharice turned her attention back toward Daniels and Davis.

"First off, you're using the term 'contacts' that you're getting information from is inaccurate. What you meant to say is your snitches," Sharice fired back. "Now that we have that cleared up, what you tryin' to offer me?"

"We can offer you safety. Get you out of the city,

set you up with a new identity. You can start life with a clean slate," Davis responded to Sharice, who smiled as though she's being sold.

"Nice. I assume all that protection comes with a price?" Sharice quipped back as Daniels nodded his head once again.

"Of course. We would need you to help us out with a little testimony," Daniels stated. "We want John Bianchi, and any other New York ties. While you're a big fish in New Orleans, we'd be willing to look past previous transgressions to put Johnny Boy away."

Sharice looked confused.

"John Bianchi?" she said as she purposely mispronounced his name. "Who is that?"

"Let's move past the part where you say you don't know who that is," Daniels said. "We've got pictures of you two meeting on several occasions."

Sharice shrugged as she continued to act as if she's puzzled.

"If you say so," she responded.

"So, I take this as you're turning down our offer?" Daniels rhetorically asked.

"Let me think," Sharice said, being a little animated, acting as though she was pondering Daniel's offer. "Live the rest of my life in some shit town where there's probably only five other black people while living on minimum wage, in a house no bigger than this room? Or rat out a guy you claim that I know, but I have no recollection of? These are my choices, right?"

Daniels chuckled once more as Sharice leaned back in her chair.

"Gee, I wish I could help you guys out because I'd love to live in some backwater city; it's always been a dream of mine. Anyway, as you can tell, I'm a little busy right now, so if you don't mind," Sharice said as she motioned the agent towards the door.

Daniels nodded his head as he and Davis made their way towards the door. Before they exited,

Daniels turned around as if he's forgotten something.

"Oh, by the way. I'm sorry to hear about your friend, Lavina," Daniels said, striking a nerve of Sharice. "Lavina James. I do believe you knew her, am I correct?"

Sharice frowned as Daniels noticed her demeanor.

"I'm sorry if I upset you in any way," Daniels said. "We've picked up the case from the locals. I'm sure with our resources, we'll be able to pick up the perp rather quickly."

Anger built in Sharice's eyes from having to relive the death of her friend.

"Good. About time y'all do some shit besides botherin' me," she snapped back. "Now get the fuck outta here," Sharice exclaimed.

Daniels and Davis both nodded their heads as they made their way out the office. Michelle was confused as she looked at a still fuming Sharice.

"Reese, what the fuck are they talkin' about?" Michelle asked. "Does this have to do with-"

"Shut the fuck up!" Sharice snapped as she jumped up from her seat, startling Michelle.

Sharice quickly picked up her phone and dialed Tracy.

"Yeah, it's me. I need you to come and sweep for bugs," she said before she hung up the line.

She turned her attention to Michelle, who still looked at her with caution.

"I'm sorry, Chelle," an apologetic Sharice said while she calmed down. "I don't trust these bitch ass feds at all. No more talking in the office until it's been swept."

Michelle nodded her head as both her and Sharice headed out of the office. As they made their way downstairs from the VIP area, Connie noticed them from the bar area and approached Sharice. She was cut off by Michelle, who had a slick grin on her face.

"Back up," Michelle replied to an enraged Connie.

"Bitch, you must be out your fuckin' mind to-"

"Enough," Sharice said to her old friend. "Do you

have my money?"

Connie shook her head as she backed down.

"I don't have the shit on me but-"

"Then don't come around until you fuckin' do," Sharice snapped as she made her way out of the club.

Michelle had a smirk on her face as she followed Sharice out of the club. A devastated Connie looked on in the brink of tears before she hardened up.

Hours later, Michelle was sitting in an SUV outside of a local restaurant observing the area and checking her phone on occasion, making sure she looked at every face that entered the establishment.

Inside the French Restaurant, Sharice and Jerome were sitting across from each other eating their meals. The restaurant was rustic in style, going for a more simplified atmosphere, with the exception of the band that provided local creole tunes for the customers.

Jerome was enjoying his meal, but can tell Sharice

wasn't in the moment.

"So, you gonna sit there and pout all day?" Jerome said, causing Sharice to drop her fork.

"I'm... I'm sorry, Rome," Sharice said. "I just got a lot of shit on my mind right now."

"I can tell," he said. "So, you wanna holla at me about it?"

"It's nothing I wanna talk about," Sharice replied.

"And there it is," Jerome snapped back, which confused his date.

"What?"

"It's the shit you used to do to me all the time. Get all quiet, and when I try and see what the deal was, you'd shut me out," Jerome answered. "Look, Kiss, I know you going through some shit, but I can be somewhat helpful with things. I'm in the game too, ya heard me. Just let me know what the deal is."

Sharice sighed as she shook her head in refusal.

"You knew what this was when you agreed to hook back up," Sharice reminded her lover. "There's just certain things I'm not gonna go into details on, whether you're in the game or not."

"So, what I hear is you don't trust me," Jerome insinuated. "I mean, if you did, you wouldn't be actin' like all this."

"Why are you doing this right now?" an irritated Sharice asked. "Why did you pick this moment to stress me over this shit?"

"I don't know, you sittin' over there like you lost your best friend and shit," Jerome said. "I mean... Reese, you know how I feel about you. I just... I don't know... I hate seeing you like this."

Sharice calmed down a bit because she knew Jerome was only trying to help. This was an attempt by her to hide once more, and not open up, which she was trying so hard not to do.

Before Sharice responded to Jerome, a Hispanic male walked over and took a seat at their table, which confused both Jerome and Sharice. He was a thin man but had expensive taste, wearing high-end clothing and an expensive watch that Sharice noticed. He had a goatee and was wearing shades which he slowly took them off, revealing a scar crossing over his left eye, leaving it discolored.

"Excuse me, may I help you?" Jerome said as the male rubbed his hand through his slicked-back hair.

"No, you can't. But your lady here most certainly can," the male said with a heavy accent as he turned his attention to Sharice.

The male's attitude enraged Jerome as he stood from his chair and became aggressive.

"Look here, nigga. I don't know what the fuck your issue is, but I'm about to-"

"Jerome! Please," Sharice said as she waved him down.

The male smiled as he looked at Sharice, who was calm.

"Smart woman," he said as Sharice waited for an explanation. "My name is Alejandro. I'm here looking for answers. Once I have what I need, you two lovely people can continue with your meal."

Jerome looked at Sharice, who continued to remain cool under pressure.

"I'm listening," she said.

"Several days ago, a shipment made its way to your docks. That shipment was later compromised. You were in contact with an associate of ours, Duval. Is this correct?" Alejandro asked.

"Yeah, we were," Sharice answered.

"Were you aware the Duval was murdered in his hotel recently?" Alejandro questioned.

"I was."

Alejandro smiled as he could tell Sharice isn't easily scared.

"You wouldn't happen to know who killed him now, would you?" he asked.

"Honestly, I thought it was your people who did the deed," Sharice responded. "I mean, we've had shit go through those docks with no issues prior to that one. Figured he fucked it up, and y'all settled up with him."

Alejandro laughed as she ran his hand through his slicked-back hair once again.

"You're right. Duval was a fuck-up. He was sloppy, which is why the shipment was compromised," he said. "The thing is, he has relatives in high places who wouldn't allow such a thing to befall him. So no, senorita, we did not have him killed. I'm here to find out who did."

Sharice looked confused.

"So, why are you asking me?" she asked. "Are you tryin' to say I had somethin' to do with that shit?"

"I thought I would start with who he was doing business with, and probably the last person to see him alive," Alejandro responded. "I mean, he compromised your docks. You would have all the motive in the world to want to see him gone."

"Yeah, but I ain't no dummy," Sharice quipped back. "I know how you Columbians operate. Even though you're in my fuckin' city, I would show respect in order to avoid any conflict between us."

A sly grin entered Alejandro's face as he leaned back in his chair.

"Is that a fact?" he said. "You see, from my understanding, this shipment was guaranteed by you. Putting two and two together, I came up with the idea that Duval was killed in order to avoid paying the debt. One from which I believe was an estimated two million dollars, am I correct?"

Sharice maintained her denial but nodded her head about one thing he said.

"That is correct. The shipment was guaranteed, but not by me. By my people," Sharice answered. "In fact, they were on their way to get with Duval to come up with a compromise in order to settle this transaction when they heard he had been killed. We never got the chance."

Alejandro tried to feel Sharice out, but she was giving him nothing to say that she was lying.

"Interesting story. I would like to talk to your

people to ask them a few questions if I may," he responded.

"You may not," a defiant Sharice quipped back. "I just told you what happened. You're not gonna go around fuckin' with my people. Look, this shit doesn't have anything to do with us. Your friend, or whatever he is, could have been killed for a thousand reasons. That's not how we operate."

Alejandro nodded his head as he rose from his seat, which made Jerome a little anxious as he stared Sharice down.

"Very well, but the debt two million dollars falls upon you," he said. "And if I find out you're lying to me... well, you know what's gonna happen, don't you?"

Sharice snickered at Alejandro's threat, which caused him to smile once more. He quickly stole a shrimp from her plate and ate it.

"Not bad. Not bad at all," he said before he bowed to Sharice. He quickly walked off as she looked at the surrounding area, and noticed three other men who had been watching their conversation from different areas of the restaurant all make their way out after him.

A frustrated Sharice grabbed her head as Jerome tried to comfort her.

"Reese, what the fuck was that?" he asked.

Sharice was silent as she took several deep breaths with her face covered. After a few moments, she raised her head and looked towards Jerome, who was still confused with everything that's going on.

"This is my life," Sharice said. "This is the type of shit I fuckin' deal with every day! You sure you wanna stick around for this?!"

Jerome initially backed away because he could tell Sharice is frustrated. He slid over to her and put his arm around her, giving her the support she needed. A normally non-affectionate Sharice succumbed to her lover's show of reassurance and rested herself upon his arm.

Later that night, back at Club Exotica, the assassin Dre and the others hired was mixed in with the crowd. As he nursed a drink at the bar area, he observed Sharice's office from below, waiting to make his move. He wore fashionable clothes to blend in with the regulars and an overcoat to conceal his weapon. He stopped to scratch his thick beard on occasion, but his eyes were fixed Sharice's office, which had the blinds down.

Inside the office, Sharice, Michelle, and James were meeting with Bull, who had a somber look on his face after he was told he needed to make a move on his friend.

"Sharice, I don't know if I can do this," Bull said.

"Bull, you're the only one who can get close to him. Trust me, if I could get anyone else to do it, I would," Sharice explained. "He tried to have me killed! He doesn't get a free pass from that shit. Look, I know this shit is difficult, and I feel you, but this has to be done. I need you to handle this shit."

Bull didn't respond as Sharice walked over to him from behind her desk and placed her hand on his shoulder.

"Take some time and get your mind straight," she advised. "After that, do what needs to be done, ya heard me?"

Bull nodded his head as he quietly got up from his chair and walked out of the office. Michelle shook her head as Sharice turned her attention towards both her and James.

"Y'all think he's gonna go through with it?" she asked.

"Shit, I wouldn't," James responded to a surprised Sharice. "I'm just sayin', you askin' a nigga to off his best friend. That's like you being told to off Connie. I know you and her are beefin' and shit now, but could you pull that trigger if Money hit you up about it?"

Sharice doesn't respond initially.

"I mean, that is fucked up, Sharice," Michelle

chimed in. "You should just let me take care of it. I know it'll be hard, but shit, you won't have any emotion behind the trigger."

"Look, I made a fuckin' decision, okay?" Sharice fired back. "Either he does what I fuckin' tell him to do, or he can be next! This isn't a fuckin' democracy! I point, you fire, it's that simple!"

James and Michelle were both surprised by Sharice's aggression, as they remained silent. Sharice calmed down as she quickly walked behind her desk to grab her jacket.

"I'm outta here. Hit me on the burner if y'all need me," she instructed before walking out of her office.

"Well, that escalated quickly," James jokingly said, which caused Michelle to burst into laughter.

Sharice made her way out of her office, which grabbed the assassin's attention as she made her way through the crowded VIP area. As she made her way down the stairs, she's stopped by Connie, who met her halfway on the staircase. Connie handed her an envelope of cash, which Sharice promptly counted before putting it in her purse. She's about to walk off when Connie stopped her once more.

"Reese, look. I know you're pissed at me, but we need to talk for real," Connie said.

"No, we don't. I've said all I needed to say to you," Sharice quipped back.

"You gonna throw all these years away for one fuckin' mistake?" Connie asked.

"Don't give me that one mistake bullshit," Sharice said as she nudged Connie out of her way.

As Sharice made her way to the bottom of the staircase, a distraught Connie looked over and noticed the assassin's locked-in stare towards Sharice as he tried to make it through the club crowd. Her eyes lit up when the assassin pulled a gun from his coat and started to raise his arm.

"Sharice!" Connie yelled before she jumped down the stairs and tackled her old friend just as the assassin opened fire. Connie was hit as screams filled the club, causing the crowd to scatter as they headed for safety or a nearby exit. Sharice pulled at Connie as she tried to cover her friend up amongst the ruckus. She was able to slide Connie's body towards the far wall when she suddenly turned around and noticed the assassin clearing the crowd with his weapon aimed for her. Sharice prepared herself for death when Michelle suddenly fired several shots from the above in VIP area, which stuck the assassin. He returned fire but was outgunned as James joined the firefight. The assassin abandoned his target and quickly headed out of the exit, with Michelle giving chase. James ran over to a distraught Sharice and protected her while he looked over the remaining crowd.

Outside the club, Michelle quickly looked around and noticed the shooter who had limped towards an alley. She quickly ran over to him and fired several more shots, which killed the assassin. As she entered the alleyway, she noticed a getaway car and driver waiting. Once the driver noticed the assassin was down, they quickly pulled off before Michelle could take a shot at them.

Michelle shook her head as she looked into the crowd and noticed a couple of Federal Agents struggling to weave their way through the crowd filled street. She quickly wiped off her gun and kicked it down a nearby storm drain before disappearing through the alley. By the time the agents arrived, they only noticed the body of the assassin. One of the agents pulled out their radio and called out to their dispatch as the other one made his way into the club.

When the agent walked into the club, James quickly dropped his gun and raised his hands. He stepped back as the agent had his gun drawn, pointing towards him. On the ground, a sobbing Sharice held her friend, who was bleeding in her arms. She looked towards the agent with desperation in her eyes.

"Call for help, please!" she cried out as the agent holstered his firearm and went onto his radio to call for help.

Sharice yelled Connie's name repeatedly as she tried to revive her friend, but received no response.

Hours later, Sharice was sitting in her office behind her desk in a dead state, still wearing her blood-covered clothes with tears streaming down her face. Her mind was circling around the events that happened earlier, tormenting her as regret filled her heart.

Tracy walked into the office with tears streaming down her face as well, when she noticed Sharice sitting behind her desk, still bloodied up.

"Sharice, I told you to come in here and change," Tracy said as she approached her friend. "You can't just sit here like this!"

Sharice doesn't respond as she's zoned out.

Tracy's words meant nothing to her. Nothing anyone could say would change her mood. Tracy walked into the office closet, pulled out an outfit for her friend, and lays it on her desk.

"Sharice, please. Clean yourself up," she said.

"I fucked up," Sharice said as she finally broke her silence.

"It's not your fault."

"What the fuck do you know?" Sharice snapped, frightening her friend. "You run a fuckin' bar! You don't know what I've done, or what I had to go through! Don't tell me it's not my fault when you don't know shit!"

Sharice rose from her seat and started to pace around the office.

"She could be dead for all I know! All the bullshit, and everything I did to her, and she saves my fuckin' life?! What kind of friend am I? Kickin' her out of my life over... over," Sharice said as she caught herself before she said anything about Lavina's death. "She could be dead, Tracy. All over some shit I started. How can you say it's not my fault?"

Tracy walked over and hugged Sharice, who started crying once more.

"I'm not part of y'all's clique or whatever, but I know that Connie knew the risks of doing what y'all do," Tracy responded. "You do too. This isn't on you. You can't blame yourself."

Sharice nodded as she backed away from her friend. She wiped her face as she tried to gather herself. Before she can respond, Michelle and Bull entered the room and noticed the state Sharice is in.

"Hey, Reese. We didn't mean to intrude," Michelle said as Sharice motioned her in.

"Don't worry about it. Spit it out," Sharice said as she awaited news from her crew.

"Well, they say Connie is gonna pull through," Michelle said, which brought relief to Sharice. "They just got her out of emergency surgery, and while it's still a little touch and go, they think she should make a full recovery."

"Thank God," a relieved Tracy responded.

Michelle was about to continue on when she stopped and looked towards Tracy, who nodded her head with understanding.

"Right. I'll be downstairs, Reese, if you need me," Tracy said as she made her way out of the office.

Once she's gone, Michelle turned her attention back towards Sharice.

"James is probably gonna have to spend a day or two locked up," Michelle said to a disappointed Sharice.

"Is his story locked in?" Sharice asked.

"Yeah, he disarmed the killer of a strap he was carryin' and was protectin' himself and you," Michelle responded. "I think they'll sweat him for a minute, but it shouldn't be nothin' too serious."

Sharice nodded her head as she turned to Bull.

"Any luck gettin' with Ritchie?" she asked.

"He's gone to the mattresses," Bull responded.

"No sign of him, Dre, or anyone one high up."

"Yeah, even Lil Dee is off in hiding," Michelle added.

Sharice sighed as anger began to build in her.

"Fine, this nigga wanna run and hide, I'm gonna cut off his supply," she said. "I want you to get a hit squad together. I want you to hit every fuckin' corner this nigga runs. I want anyone associated with this nigga dropped! He thinks he can take a shot at me and Connie and still earn, he's out his fuckin' mind."

Both Bull and Michelle were stunned by their leader's aggressiveness.

"Sharice, maybe we wanna think this through," Bull cautioned. "I mean, we need to get you to safety before they decide-"

"Fuck safety!" Sharice exclaimed. "I'm gonna be on these streets lookin' for his bitch ass! I ain't hiding! He wants to fuck with me, then I'm ready to roll, for real!"

Michelle and Bull nodded their heads. Sharice

had a look in her eyes they had never seen before. Before they could respond, Jerome burst into the office and noticed Sharice and the blood covering her clothing.

"Sharice?! Are you okay?" he said as he quickly approached her.

"I'm fine. I'm fine, it's not my blood," Sharice assured him.

"What the fuck happened? Is this because of that Columbian asshole from earlier?" Jerome asked, which surprised Bull.

"Columbian? What Columbian? One of the friends of the guy from that night?" Bull asked, being careful not to say specifics.

"No. Well, yes. Fuck! Look, y'all just give me a sec. Chelle, bring the car around. I wanna go check up on Connie after I clean myself up a bit. Do a few rounds around the block to see if you see anything," a frustrated Sharice said.

Michelle and Bull nodded, and both of them

headed out of the office. Sharice turned her attention to a concerned Jerome.

"Look, I don't really have time to do this now. Connie got shot protecting me of all things, and she's outta surgery, so I'm gonna change and visit her," Sharice said as she tried to walk off.

Jerome pulled her back by her arm, because her brief explanation did not satisfy him.

"What?"

"Reese, what's going on?" he asked.

"I just told you what's going on, Rome. What the fuck else do you wanna know?" she asked him and Jerome realized that was all the information he was going to get from her.

"Fuck it, I guess nothin'," Jerome said as he released his hold on Sharice.

She grabbed the outfit Tracy had laid out for her earlier and was about to head out of the office when she turned and looked at Jerome. She knew he was just trying to help and was doing what any other man would do in his position. She finally softened up as she addressed him.

"Rome, I... let's hook up later tonight. Your place. I'll... I'll tell you everything you wanna know," Sharice said.

Jerome looked at Sharice and could tell she was in pain. He slowly nodded his head as he walked over to the office door and opened it for her. Sharice forced a slight smile on her face as she walked out of the office. As she made her way down the VIP stairs to the main floor, she had several flashbacks of the attack that wounded her friend. Sadness filled her eyes as she slowly made her way towards the bathroom area.

Chapter 6

Plan of Action

Several hours later, after the club shooting, Michelle's vehicle pulled up to the local hospital and Sharice exited the passenger side. As she walked up, she noticed Money Mike smoking a cigarette just outside of the building. She sighed as she walked over towards him.

"The fuck you doin' here?" a direct Sharice asked.

Money smiled as he approached her and gave her an awkward hug.

"I'm sorry, boo. 'Bout your friend," he said as he backed away from her. "How you doin'?"

"I'm good, but that doesn't answer my question

on why the fuck you here," she stated.

"Connie got shot, shit," he responded. "Can't I come visit and check on the wellbein' of someone who works for me?"

"First, she works for me, not you," Sharice corrected. "Second, you never even liked her. If it was up to you, you woulda shot her a long time ago, so what the fuck, Money?"

Money chuckled as he dropped the concerned act.

"Well, you work for me, so by extension, she works for me," he responded. "And you right, I ain't never liked her bad-tempered ass, but I do like you. So, if you strugglin', then I'm gonna struggle, ya heard me."

Sharice isn't impressed as she folded her arms.

"Seems like you got a lot goin' on and shit. That fuckin' shootin' made the news," Money said.

"It's niggas killin' niggas. It won't play for long," Sharice responded.

"Either way, violence on the TV causes concerns

for a few interested parties. Now, I know that's your girl and shit, and I know you not as fuckin' throwed as she is, but I don't want no more shit to go down," Money responded to a shocked Sharice.

"Are you fuckin' serious?!" she asked.

"Dead serious," Money responded sternly. "I know you wanna go all G.I. Jane and start smokin' niggas, and normally, I wouldn't blame you. But it's an election year, and the niggas who allow us to run the city don't need unnecessary blood fillin' the streets. I know you and that nigga Dre wanna battle it out, but that shit ain't gonna happen."

Sharice was amazed as her frustration continued to build with each moment.

"He shot my fuckin' friend, Mike!" Sharice responded loudly. "That nigga doesn't get a pass for that shit!"

"First of all, lower your fuckin' voice," Money snapped back. "I know you a little emotional right now, so I'm gonna let that slide. Now, what happened to your girl is unfortunate, but I'm hearin' you the reason this beef started in the first fuckin' place."

Sharice didn't respond as she tried to keep it together in front of her boss.

"Not to sound like a broken record, but this is the type of shit why I never supported you for boss. You let your emotions get in the way, and now your girl up in the hospital shot and shit. A thousand ways you coulda handled this, but since you don't have balls to handle this shit, I will. I'm gonna send word to that nigga. I'm gonna see if we can arrange a sitdown."

A stunned Sharice had heard enough.

"A sitdown? Fuck this shit! I'm not sittin' down with the nigga who shot my girl!" Sharice exclaimed.

"Look, you shot him; he shot her," Money responded. "I say y'all are even right now. Let that shit go, and we can-"

"I ain't lettin' go shit! I'm gonna pop this nigga my fuckin' self!" an enraged Sharice responded.

"I then told you to watch your fuckin' tone with

me," a hardened Money responded as he and Sharice stared at each other toe to toe. "Now that's the way the shit gonna be, ya heard me? I ain't askin' for shit. Once I set this shit up, you gonna bring yo' ass there, look pretty, and shut the fuck up! Or we can handle the other way. Your choice?"

Sharice didn't back down but knew she was in a bad situation. To take on a Faction Boss was a losing battle, and Sharice knew it. With her pride hurt, she slowly backed away from Money.

"I figured you'd choose right," he responded, calming down as well. "I ain't sayin' y'all niggas gotta be friends and shit, but this back and forth, it's over."

Sharice didn't respond once more, still fuming over having to sit down with her enemy.

"I know it's fucked up, but hey, it is what it is right now," Money said. "I'm gonna make sure we get that nigga in line though, for real."

An unconvinced Sharice rolled her eyes. She was about to walk off into the hospital when Money called out to her.

"Hey, Reese. I really am sorry about your girl," he said as he tried to reach out to her.

His words were ignored as she walked into the hospital without a response.

Connie was located on the second level of the ICU unit. She laid in bed unconscious and hooked to various machines that were monitoring her. Seated next to her at her bedside was Rose, who looked on, watching Connie quietly. When she heard the door opening, she put on the emotional, concerned act, looking like she was on the brink of tears.

Sharice was caught off guard when she noticed Rose sitting next to her friend. She walked over and observed a concerned Rose.

"You must be the new girl," Sharice said to a startled Rose.

"I'm the only girl," Rose said with an attitude as she looked towards Sharice as if she didn't know who she was. "And you are?"

"I'm Sharice."

Rose acted surprised as she changed her tone.

"Oh my god, I'm so sorry," she said. "I...I didn't know. Hey, I'm Rose. Connie told me all about you. I thought you were... well..."

"I know. No worries," Sharice said as she walked over to her friend and observed her.

Sharice struggled to keep her emotions together as a few tears made their way down her face. To see her friend in that state scared her. Rose offered her a Kleenex, which Sharice took.

"Thank you," she responded.

"No thanks needed. I'm on my second box," Rose replied as Sharice took a seat next to her and Connie.

"Have the doctors been in yet?" Sharice asked.

"Yeah. They said she's looking good, but she hasn't responded yet," Rose answered. "I couldn't believe it."

"Were you there when it happened?" Sharice

asked.

"No, I was at my crib. One of my friends was there and had called me when it went down. By the time I made it over, the ambulance had already pulled off. Shit, they just let me in here after I acted a fool. Talkin' about family only. I'm like I'm her fuckin' family, ya know."

Sharice chuckled as she looked towards Connie and all the machines she was connected to.

"How did it come to this?" she said. "She tell you that me and her had a fallin' out?"

Rose nodded her head as she silently looked on.

"All the shit we been through, and she still saves my life. I should be the one laid up in that bed, or dead probably," Sharice said as sadness entered her eyes. "All this trippin' over bullshit, and the girl saves my life. You can't get more loyal than that."

"I haven't been with her long, but the one thing I got from her was loyalty," Rose shared. "I mean, don't get me wrong, she can go a little wild and shit, but when it came down to it, I can tell her truest thoughts. She really loved you. It's all she would talk about at times. I feel like I already know you."

Sharice smiled as she looked over her friend.

"Yeah, me and Cee go way back. Had our lil' crew since high school. I already lost one of our group not too long ago," Sharice responded. "I don't wanna lose another one."

"Yeah, I heard. Sorry for your loss," Rose said to a surprised Sharice.

"You know about that?" she asked.

"Yeah. Like I said, Connie talked about you all the time. She said y'all lost y'all friend growing up. I think her name was Ladonna, Louvinia, or something like that," Rose said.

"Lavina."

"Yeah, that was it. I could tell she was a little tore up about her death. She told me you took it kinda hard as well," Rose responded as Sharice looked at her a little suspiciously.

"Yeah, it was rough on me. Connie would never admit it, but I know she was strugglin' with it too. They used to date way back when, and I don't think she ever got over that," Sharice replied with false information.

"Yeah, I could tell," Rose responded. "I mean, she didn't want to talk about it, but I could tell she was hurting. They say you never get over a true love. Maybe she never got over Lavina."

Sharice realized that Rose isn't who she seemed to be after that comment. She looked back at Connie and nodded her head while she kept her thoughts to herself.

"Maybe she didn't," Sharice responded. "Anyway, I can see she's in good hands right now. I'll leave you two alone."

Sharice rose from her chair and shook Rose's hand.

"Rose, right?" she said as Rose nodded, confirming. "It's not Rose Hernandez, is it? I remember Connie tellin' me some stories about you."

"Oh no, it's Rose Solis," Rose answered. "I don't want you puttin' nobody else's gossip on me."

Sharice smiled as she nodded her head.

"I stand corrected. Well, it was nice to meet you, Rose."

"Nice to meet you as well."

Sharice smiled once more before she made her way out of the room. Her smile dropped as she quickly picked up her phone and dialed Diego on her line. As she reached the elevator, he finally answered.

"Yeah, it's me. I need you to do a check on a Rose Solis for me," she said as she entered the elevator.

It was nighttime and a stressed out Sharice sat on Jerome's couch, sipping a glass of wine as Jerome massaged her feet. He was a little stunned after Sharice told him everything he wanted to know as promised.

"And that's pretty much it," she said before she

finished off her glass.

"Shit," Jerome responded, speechless with everything she had just told him. "So, what's the plan?"

"Plan? There is no plan. Right now, I have the Columbian on my ass for two mi

l, my homegirl lyin' in the bed hanging on by a thread because of me, and I can't do anything to the niggas that did it because my boss wants to sit down. On top of all that, I'm supposed to be getting' shit straight for Houston. What kind of plan fixes all that?" Sharice asked.

"Well, when you say it like that," Jerome said as Sharice finally cracked a smile.

"I know. It's fucked up," Sharice said. "I just feel so fuckin' helpless right now."

"The Sharice I know wouldn't let that stop her," Jerome said. "I mean, this is the girl who took control of the block by usin' her head. You was hungry, had a goal, and went at it."

"Yeah, I get that, but it's not the same. There's-"

"Nothing has changed," Jerome interrupted. "The game is still the game, and last I checked, wasn't nobody out there as bad as you. The thing is, you had a vision, a dream so to speak, on what you wanted to do, and you took that bitch. On the cool, I just think you got complacent with shit."

Sharice was impressed as she reached over to the nearby coffee table and poured herself another glass of wine.

"I have to admit, maybe you're right," she said. "Maybe I have gotten a little soft since steppin' back from the streets. I guess when you get the shit you battled for, you stop takin' risks because you don't wanna lose it. The old me wouldn't have settled for this shit."

"Exactly. I mean, come on, Kiss, I know you got it in you to handle this shit. Trust me, I'm the nigga who has the most to lose here, and I think you should fight," Jerome said to a confused Sharice.

"You have the most to lose?"

"Yeah."

"How?"

Jerome paused for a moment as he released Sharice's foot from his grasp.

"I think either way I'm gonna lose you," he explained. "If the worst happens, and you get popped, or arrested, or some shit like that, I lose you. If you win, take out all your enemies, and end up on top, I still lose you. I'd be able to see you rise, which is cool, but either way, we both know this shit here is on borrowed time."

Sharice sighed as she put down her wine glass.

"Rome, look. I know what happened when I got my stripes," Sharice said. "I was young back then. A whole lot has changed."

"Has it? I'm just sayin' I know you, Kiss. Once you become boss, it's gonna be I don't have time for this, it makes me look weak or whatever. I mean, come on. You honestly think that once you achieve that shit that you gonna wanna keep this shit going?" Jerome said.

"Yes! Because after that, I've achieved everything I set out to achieve," Sharice responded. "I will be the boss, and as such can do whatever the fuck I want. Appearance and shit won't matter then."

"'Til the next big thing comes around," Jerome responded. "When you was young, all you thought about was runnin' your own corner, and you did that. Then all you thought about was running several corners, you did that. Next, it was becomin' captain of a crew, which you did, and finally, your goal was to run a city and be an underboss, and that's where we are now. Every time you shoot for somethin' and get it, you look towards the next thing, and by doing so, sacrifice relationships to get it."

"But there isn't anything else to get after this," Sharice replied. "This is the ultimate goal. I mean, seriously, what's after boss?"

"I don't know. Shit, super boss," Jerome joked,

causing Sharice to laugh. "I mean, whatever it is it won't take you long before you're doing what you need to get that shit. I just don't think me and you will ever settle in, you dig?"

Sharice sighed as she pondered for a few moments.

"I'm trying to change Rome, for real," Sharice admitted. "I'm not sayin' it's gonna be easy, but I really am tryin'. Look, I can't promise you what the future will hold, 'cause you right, I'm always tryin' to push forward, but on the real, I'm really wantin' us to work in the long run. However, if this isn't in either of our futures, then we need to quit wastin' time fussin' about it, and enjoy the time we have together."

Jerome slowly nodded his head with agreement as he moved over and kissed her. The two started to get hot and heavy with each other as Jerome unbuttoned Sharice's shirt. She started to undress him as well as the couch became their sexual haven for the moment.

In an apartment complex located in the New Orleans East, Michelle was in James' apartment bedroom mounted on top of him in his bed as she grinded on him nonstop, which drove him wild. The apartment was decked out for the neighborhood it was in, with expensive furniture, appliances, and electronics. It's a typical bachelor pad without a woman's touch as there were no decorations whatsoever in the place. The windows were covered with sheets, and there wasn't much organization in the apartment.

Michelle continued to instill her will on James as she rode him to the brink of orgasm. James tried to fight back and hold her off, but in the end, she proved to be too much as he finally let out a moan and several grunts, letting her know that she had won the sexual battle they were having. An evil smile entered her face as she began grinding him harder, which drove James wild as he begged her to stop. His pleas only made her go harder. James had finally had enough and pushed her to the side of the bed, much to her delight.

"Bitch, you fuckin' crazy," he said, panting, trying to catch his breath.

"Nigga, please. You said you could handle that shit," Michelle said with a smile on her face as she faced him. "I can see you just like any other nigga. All talk."

She quickly reached down and stroked his manhood. James reacted quickly, removing her hand from his body and jumped out of bed, causing her to laugh.

"What the fuck is wrong with you?" James said. Michelle got comfortable in the bed while she looked at him.

"I told you that you weren't ready for me. Shit, I held back a lot, and your ass already actin' like I'm too much for ya," she said while James located his underwear and put them back on.

"Girl whatever. I could handle it," he replied as he got back in the bed and under the covers. "I was just caught off guard a little, that's all. I seen what you got, and I just need to change it up a bit, that's all."

"Whatever, nigga," Michelle said, giggling as she reached for her phone and checked the time. "Fuck! I didn't realize it was that late. Let me get my ass up outta here."

Before she's able to get out of the bed, James grabbed her arm and pulled her back in.

"Why you runnin' off. Why don't you stay the night?" he asked.

"What? This pussy then got you wantin' me to stay the night? I thought you was better than that," Michelle joked as she finally rose from the bed and began getting dressed.

"I'm just sayin', why is your runnin' home to that nigga? I mean, what kind of name is Theo anyway? Fuckin' Cosby Show ass nigga," James mocked, which caused Michelle to laugh.

"Theo is my man, and unlike some I know, can handle all of me," Michelle quipped back.

"So, it's all about the dick?" James asked.

"Nah, it's more, but that's neither here nor there," Michelle said as she put on her socks and tennis shoes. "This was fun, and I wouldn't mind makin' you beg again 'cause it's cute, but if you gonna start catchin' feelings and all…"

"It's not catchin' feelings and shit. I just wanna lay with you. Is that so much to ask?" James responded.

"Man, I swear I'm sittin' here soundin' like the nigga, and you sittin' here soundin' like the bitch. Should I leave forty on the dresser when I leave out?" Michelle mocked with a laugh.

"I fuckin' hate you," James playfully said.

"Yeah well, your dick said otherwise," Michelle said as she mounted him once more before she kissed him passionately.

She hopped out of bed soon after and grabbed her

keys and her cigarettes before she headed out of the apartment, leaving James wanting more of her.

As she exited the apartment, she took a moment and lit a cigarette, looking around the area. She's about to walk off when something captured her eyes. She was stunned as she noticed Dre walking with a female, making their way into another building in the apartment complex. She quietly observed the two who were laughing and conversing as they made their way into one of the nearby apartments. As soon as they were inside, Michelle quickly made her way down the stairwell of James' apartment building and up the stairwell of the apartment building that Dre and the female went into. She took a look at the apartment number and quietly placed her ear to the door to see if she heard anything.

After a few moments, she slowly backed away, rushed down the stairs and headed to her car. She quickly picked up her phone and dialed Sharice's number while going into her glove box to pull out her gun.

Sharice was asleep in Jerome's bed when her phone started to ring. She was finally awakened by the phone, reached over to the nearby nightstand, and answered it.

"Hello," a groggy Sharice answered.

"Hey, it's me. Remember that gift you was lookin' for. I just happen to come across it."

"And what gift was that?" Sharice asked as she wiped her eyes.

"The big one. The main one. The one that would make us all very happy," Michelle responded on the phone as Sharice looked confused.

"The across the border gift?" she asked.

"No, the other gift, the local one," Michelle responded.

"Chelle, I have no idea what you're talkin' about," Sharice responded as she yawned.

"The big one! The... the uptown one! You know!

The-"

"Alright, alright, I got you, I think," Sharice responded, finally catching on. "I thought I told y'all not to worry about that right now. That I'm still price checkin'."

"Yeah, I know that, but since it was here, and I'm here, I figured why not just buy it," Michelle stated as Sharice pondered her options for several moments.

"No, just... just leave it. I think I have a better way to buy it," Sharice said. "Meet me at the club tomorrow at noon. You think we'll be able to make a purchase at this spot in the future, or do you think the sale won't last?"

"Hard to tell," Michelle responded. "I mean, it seems hopeful, but I'm not sure. I got the credit card all ready to make the purchase. Just say the word."

Sharice sighed because she would love nothing more than to give the order for Dre's demise, but because she was ordered to let it go by her boss, Money, her hands were tied for the moment.

"No, not tonight," Sharice said. "We'll discuss it tomorrow."

Sharice hung up the phone, thinking for a few moments. She started sending out a series of texts trying to get confirmation on a few things before she ultimately laid back down in the bed to turn in for the night.

At the FBI monitoring station, Agent Flores walked in with a smile on her face, noticing Daniels and Davis looking at her as soon as she comes in.

"Hey. What's up?" she asked.

"We're pulling you out," Davis responded to a stunned Rose.

"Pulling me out? Why?"

"You were made," Davis answered. "We received a search hit on your name from the NOPD's database. Someone did a search for Rose Solis, and your name hit back into our system."

"So, I thought the whole point for the system was

when the locals notice that they were not to respond. Just signifying that I was undercover. Why is that so bad?" Flores asked as she tried to understand.

"Well, the officer in question who made the request, Officer Diego, is on the Faction's payroll for one," Daniels answered, which stunned Flores.

"Oh shit," she replied as she took a seat.

"It's not all bad news," Davis responded. "We're going to go ahead and pull Diego. We have him on several criminal charges, but with an interfering with a federal investigation charge, we can ball all that up and put him away for twenty plus years."

"Unless he agrees to testify on our behalf at Sharice's RICO trial," Daniels said. "If we can get him to flip, we could bust open this whole thing."

"Well, if he's in custody, then I'm not burned," Flores said.

"That's if he hasn't told anyone," Davis pointed out. "And we can't confirm if he has or hasn't. Right now, it's just safer to pull you."

Flores lowered her head with disgust while Daniels approached her.

"Hey, don't sweat it. You did good work out there," he said to comfort her.

"Why is he looking into me?" Flores asked.

"We're not sure," said Davis while Flores thought to herself silently for few moments before she snapped her fingers.

"That fucking Sharice! I know it's got to be her," she responded. "I must have said something to her that got her checking me out."

"You spoke with Sharice?" Daniels asked.

"Yeah. I was going to tell you this morning that me and her had a conversation. Nothing worthwhile, but she is feeling guilty about Connie getting shot. She said Connie saved her life that night, which I take it means that she was the target. They may take another crack at her, or she might take a shot at them," Flores said.

"We're trying to control that, but I can see it

getting out of hand," Daniels said. "Increased surveillance hours were approved after the shooting. We have locals teaming up with agents to run and operate the surveillance. I can't see either side being able to make a move before we know about it."

"Yeah, but like you said, she's smart. She always has a plan," Flores reminded the agents. "I mean, she's really in her feelings right now. Why not take another crack at her? Let's see if the near-death experience has changed her attitude about things. She's carrying the weight of her best friend's shooting right now. We may never see her this vulnerable again."

Daniels and Davis looked at each other as Davis shrugged.

"Okay. We'll pay her another visit. Get on the phone with the club team, and tell them to let us know when she arrives. Meantime, you're in house for the time being," Daniels said to a disappointed Flores.

"Daniels, I think you're blowing this out of proportion. If we pick up Diego quickly, I'm sure we can save-"

"Sorry, Flores. I'm not willing to risk it. You've done a good job, but for now, you're on desk patrol," Daniels answered.

Flores sighed as she nodded her head with understanding. Daniels and Davis quickly made their way out of the station. Flores took a seat by a nearby computer, pulled out her cell phone, and dialed the club surveillance team as she was instructed.

At the club, Sharice was at her desk in her office working on some documents, when Michelle walked into the office and greeted her.

"Hey, am I early?" she asked when she noticed that it's just her and Sharice in the office.

"No, them other fools are late as always," Sharice said. "Guess that military training never goes away since you're the only one who is ever on time for shit.

Pull up a chair."

Michelle chuckled as she took a seat across from her boss as Sharice leaned back in her chair

"So, I assume you were talking about Dre last night?" Sharice asked.

Michelle nodded her head, confirming.

"Where'd you see him at?"

"In the east. He was walkin' with some girl up in an apartment in Huntington Park," she responded, catching Sharice's attention.

"Did you say Huntington Park?"

"Yeah, why?"

"Doesn't James live there?" a suspicious Sharice asked.

"Well, yeah."

"So, what were you doing there?"

Michelle seemed a little uneasy with the line of questioning she's receiving.

"I was... well... what does that matter?" she responded. "I mean, I saw the nigga there, that's all

I'm talkin' about."

Sharice was stunned as a smile grew on her face.

"You and James are fucking, aren't you?" she replied to an embarrassed Michelle.

"No! Well, kinda... I mean, I wasn't there for that specifically," Michelle stuttered.

"Oh my God," Sharice said as she got comfortable in her chair. "When did this start?"

"I mean, do we really need to talk about this? I thought we were talkin' about Dre and how to handle that," Michelle said as she tried to deflect the conversation.

"Well, I didn't know all this shit was goin' on," Sharice joked. "I mean, I thought you had a nigga you was good with. Come on, girl. Out with the details."

Michelle sighed, knowing Sharice wasn't going to let it go.

"I mean, it wasn't like I was lookin' for it," Michelle said. "I mean y'all got me all up in this boy's face workin' with him and shit. I don't know. I mean, he needed a ride from lock up after he was released; we got to talkin' about shit on the ride to his spot. He invites me up, and the next thing I know, we was in his room fucking."

Sharice was intrigued by this tale, while Michelle was still a little embarrassed.

"I've always wondered. Is he any good?" Sharice asked as Michelle looked at her with amazement.

"Are you serious?" Michelle replied. "I mean, no disrespect, but don't you think that's a bit much? I mean, how would you feel if I asked you how good Jerome is in bed?"

"Girl, that's fuckin' different, and you know it," Sharice pointed. "If I was askin' about your house boo, then you would have a point. Unless you sayin' that James is a little more than a side nigga."

Michelle didn't respond, and Sharice noticed her questions may be getting to her.

"You know what? You're right. My bad, I apologize. I didn't mean to pry, it just caught me off guard," Sharice said as she backed down.

Michelle smiled and shook her head.

"I'm not gonna go into details, but he has potential," she said, which once again captured Sharice's interest. "He definitely has the equipment to make shit work, let me tell you."

"Oh yeah?"

"Yeah. It's very, very-"

Michelle's story was interrupted as Tracy walked into the office.

"Hey. Look, I'm sorry to interrupt you, but those feds you spoke with the other day, they're back," she said. "They don't have a warrant or anything but are requesting to speak with you again. I was about to tell them to leave like you told me before, but with everything that happened, I figured I'd ask. You want me to send them up?"

"Nah," Sharice said as she got up from her seat. "I'll go down and meet them."

Tracy nodded and made her way out of the office

as Sharice peeked down through the blinds onto the main floor and noticed Daniels and Davis looking around.

"Hang back here," Sharice said to Michelle. "They might be looking for you. Keep watch from up here. If you see me stretch my arm out like this in the air, get the fuck out."

Michelle nodded her head, positioning herself to look down towards the main floor as Sharice walked out of the office to greet the agents.

"Gentlemen, we meet again," Sharice said as she approached the agents.

"Hello, Ms. Legget. I'm sorry we're not meeting under better circumstances. Can we talk for a moment?" Agent Daniels asked.

Sharice nodded as she lead them over to a nearby table where all three took a seat across from each other.

"How's Constance doing?" Daniels asked.

"Seems like she's gonna make it. Of course, you

already knew that, I assume, so can we cut the bullshit and y'all tell me why y'all are here this time?" a blunt Sharice responded.

Daniels nodded his head and he went into the reason he's there.

"From what I understand, the shooter wasn't here aiming for Constance. It wasn't random or anything. It seems that they were aiming for you," he responded. "I think it's safe to say that the shooter missed their mark, and there may be another attempt on your life."

"Well, that's nothing new," Sharice replied.

"True, but they almost achieved their goal," Davis chimed in. "And not only did they miss you, but they shot your friend. So, my question is, what happens if they come back for you?"

Sharice chuckled as she shook her head in disbelief.

"Now, why would someone come after a businesswoman such as myself?" she asked.

"Let's cut the bullshit as you said," Daniels fired back. "We both know what you're into and how you make a living. Eventually, you're going to have to answer for that life by either us or the streets. I know you're big and bad, but the real question isn't how you'll react when they attack you, but how many more people are willing to get shot, or worse yet, die because of you?"

Sharice was silent because Daniels caught her off guard. His words truly bothered her as she thought about Lavina's death, and Connie's shooting among countless others she held in her heart. He had struck a nerve with her when she noticed both Bull and James making their way into the club.

"I... I think it's time for you to go," Sharice said as she got up from her seat.

"It doesn't have to be like this, Sharice. We can protect you," Daniels said.

Sharice didn't respond as she walked off and headed back up to her office. Bull and James followed as Daniels and Davis finally got up from their chairs as well.

"Well, that hit her hard," Davis said.

"Yeah. Rattled the cage with that one," his partner replied as both men headed out of the club.

An aggravated Sharice stormed in her office and sat behind her desk as her crew looked on with concern.

"Hey, you okay?" Michelle inquired.

"Yeah. Fuckin' feds and their mind games, that's all," Sharice said as she calmed down.

Before she can speak further, she received a call on her burner phone and quickly answered. After a few words, she hung up the line with a smile on her face.

"That was perfect timing," she said as she addressed her crew. "As you all know, Mike shut us down with the Dre war. He'd rather kiss that nigga's ass than go toe to toe with him. Said it's an election year and blah, blah, blah. The thing is, that don't sit right with me, so I'm gonna move against these niggas anyway."

Michelle had an evil smirk on her face as she nodded her head with approval. James nodded his head, approving. Bull, however, was the opposite of the other two.

"All due respect, but are you sayin' you're goin' against the boss' orders?" he asked.

"Yes. Mike isn't close to the streets anymore. His life consists of collecting money, fucking hoes, and stuntin' in his limo. He's lost his way," Sharice said. "Nobody takes a shot at me and gets off the hook. That nigga was dead when he set that up, he just didn't know it yet. I have a plan, and if it goes down, I'll take out Dre and get that fuckin' Columbian off my ass. I know you're a by the rules type of dude, Bull, so you can bail out if you wanna, but I really could use you on this."

Bull looked around and was still on the fence.

Sharice waited for his approval, but eventually moved on when he hesitated.

"First thing's first, can either of you drive a big rig?" Sharice asked.

Michelle raised her hand.

"Yeah, I can. Used to move those rigs in the military, so I know how to handle them," she said.

"Good. You, and... James. I want y'all two to head to Baton Rouge tomorrow morning," Sharice said.

"Baton Rouge? What's out there," James asked.

A smile entered Sharice's face as she began to describe what her plan was. Both James and Michelle were into the details as a conflicted Bull looked on with concern.

Ritchie was driving down the freeway when his cell phone began to ring. He checked the caller ID, and answered it via the Bluetooth in his car.

"Bull, hey. Didn't expect to hear from you any time soon," he said. "Is your girl bustin' your balls for that hit on her?"

"Look, Ritchie, I didn't call you for all that. I wanna know... is... is there still an opening for me in your future plans?" Bull asked as a cryptic smile grew on Ritchie's face.

"I don't know. What happened?" he asked.

"Sharice is about to make a move on your boy. Money told her not to move, but she's doin' her own thing now. She's outta control. Without rules, this thing doesn't mean anythin'," said Bull, much to Ritchie's satisfaction.

"So, you're finally jumpin' off the broad's tit, I see," Ritchie responded. "You know I'll take care of ya. So tell me, what does the bookyak have in store for my man?"

Ritchie continued to listen to Bull's words as he drove down the freeway with a big smile on his face, happy that his friend had finally come around.

Chapter 7

Come at the Empress, You Best Not Miss

In a typical truck stop just outside of Baton Rouge, Michelle and James pulled up in the parking lot in an older broken down car. James made sure he blocked the only lane out of the stop before he shut the car down. He turned and admired Michelle, who was wearing really short shorts, a revealing top t-shirt with heels on, and sunglasses. She was sitting on the passenger side, looking in the mirror as she worked on her makeup.

"I'm tellin' you this shit ain't gonna work," he said as Michelle flipped up the mirror.

"Nigga, stop. I've been doing shit like this for a

while. Just let me be great for once," she said.

"Aight, Ms. Great. Good luck with all that," he responded as he exited the car. Michelle exited the vehicle as well as she lifted the car's hood and acted as though she was checking out the motor.

Several minutes later, an eighteen-wheeler pulled up and was trying to vacate the area, but was blocked by Michelle and the supposedly broken down car. He honked his horn, attempting to get Michelle's attention, who was bending over towards the hood, making sure the driver could see every aspect of her body. The driver became frustrated as he lowered the window.

"Hey, move that piece of shit out of the way," he yelled with a strong southern accent.

Michelle smiled as she turned and faced the eighteen-wheeler. The male driving was an older redneck type, complete with a long beard covering his face. He also wore a trucker hat over his head and was annoyed with Michelle blocking his exit at the moment.

"Hey, cutie. So, what had happened was my ride then broke down, and it won't start," Michelle said with a ratchet accent. "Is there any way you can help me out, baby?"

"The fuck do I look like AutoZone?" the red neck responded. "Just push the shit to the side so I can get out!"

"I tried, but it won't move. I don't think I'm strong enough. Can you give me a push, please?" Michelle said as she tried to attract the driver.

The driver didn't fall for her flirtation but got out of his rig nevertheless to help move the disabled vehicle to the side.

"Let's hurry this up," he said as he went to the back of the car.

Michelle noticed his swastika tattoo on his arm as he attempted to push the vehicle, but was unable to.

"Is the fucking thing in neutral?" he asked.

A ditzy Michelle slapped her head and laughed.

"Well, duh. Why didn't I think of that?" she said, re-entering the car.

Before the red neck can respond, James came out from hiding and swung his gun to the back of his head, knocking him out cold. He looked at Michelle and laughed as she folded her arms with an attitude.

"What I told you?" he gloated. "These are Aryans. They ain't gonna fuck with no hood bitch like yourself. Don't care how fine you think you is."

"Nigga, move this fool so we can check out the truck," Michelle said she popped the trunk of the run-down car.

The two dumped the redneck in the trunk and closed it. Michelle quickly started the car and parked it out of the way of the eighteen-wheeler. James grabbed the keys and unlocked the trailer attached to the rig and was stunned when he opened it up.

"This can't all be heroin. Ain't no way," James said as Michelle hopped into the back of the trailer and noticed several bags mixed in with the cargo.

She opened one bag, pulled out stacks of Euros, and tossed some to James with a smile on her face. James looked at it, confused.

"What the fuck kinda money is this shit," he asked.

"It's Euros. Ain't you ever been anywhere?" Michelle asked.

"Eur-what?"

"It's the money they use in Europe. It's worth a shit load more than our money," she explained. "Wonder if Sharice knew that?"

"I don't know, but what I do know is we gotta long trip back, and we're gonna be carryin' a lot of dope, so let's get this shit outta here before someone comes lookin' for it," James responded as he handed the cash back to Michelle.

Michelle nodded as she returned the cash to the bag and jumped out of the trailer so James could close the doors. Once the trailer was secure, Michelle jumped in the driver's side of the truck, as James entered into the passenger side. He immediately frowned as the stench of the cabin disgusted him.

"Filthy white muthafucka," he said as he lowered the window.

Michelle laughed as she shifted the rig and slowly pulled out of the truck stop. As they cleared the area, Michelle playfully yanked the cord, causing the horn to honk. James was confused with Michelle's actions as they made their way towards New Orleans.

J Rock, Danky, Dre, and a few others were at their normal meeting spot on the lakefront area when Ritchie pulled up and made his way over towards them. He had a smile on his face, excited with the news he has to share. Dre seemed irritated. He was the first to acknowledge Ritchie's arrival.

"Yo, man, what the fuck?" he said. "We've been waiting here like forty-five minutes and shit!"

"There was an accident on the freeway. What do you want from me?" Ritchie said as he took a seat with the others.

"To fuckin' be somewhere when you supposed to, shit! We all out in the open and shit. All we need is that bitch's people to see us, and run up," Dre said to an unbothered Ritchie.

"Well, she's not gonna be a problem for long," Ritchie teased, catching everyone's attention. "I know where she's gonna be at. You can end this shit by tonight!"

"What you then heard?" an interested Danky asks.

"There's a shipment they're unloading in a warehouse uptown. It's a big score from what I heard. They've been short on supply ever since Miami has been compromised, so to keep the shit flowing, they got their hands on a shipment," Ritchie explained.

Dre was unimpressed with the news.

"Nigga, how does that help us?" he said. "Ain't no way she goes there herself."

"That's just it, she is. If there is any issues with this shit, the Faction could be cleaned out. How long you think they're gonna last without product?" Ritchie said. "You know how this broad is. She's hands-on. My guy said she's gonna be there to oversee the shipment. Her and all of management. The thing is, she'll be with around ten to fifteen soldiers as well. I know it's risky, but we can send what we have at her and end the bitch's life. You do want to end this thing, right?"

Dre pondered for a moment, trying to decide the next move. J Rock was thinking as well.

"Aye, I don't know 'bout y'all, but I'm losin' money out the ass 'cause of this war," he said. "I say we take our chances and take out the bitch while we can. We all got shooters there that can battle it out."

"Yeah, but there's too many unknowns and shit. Plus, how we know the bitch is even gonna be there? I mean, I know what your man said, but can you really trust that? You willin' to go in that bitch blind?" Dre said, giving the others things to think about.

"Why don't we send someone there to case the block out?" Danky suggested. "Soon as they spot ol' girl, make the call, and we end the shit."

Ritchie nodded his head as they waited for Dre's response.

"Aight, I can run with that," Dre said as he turned to Lil Dee, who was down by the car and waved him over.

Lil Dee rushed over to meet with his cousin and the others.

"What's up?"

"Aye, I need you to stake out a joint, and hit us up if you see ol' girl arriving," Dre said to a disappointed Lil Dee.

"What the fuck? Am I gonna be waiting around all day and shit," he responded. "I got shit to do, nigga, damn."

"Nigga, fuck your plans," Dre fired back. "We tryin' to end this war and shit. All you need to do is check out this warehouse uptown, and hit us up when she rolls through!"

Lil Dee sighed as he backed down and nodded his head. Dre waved him off, causing him to head back towards the car.

"Niggas always complain' and shit," Dre said, turning his attention back to the crew. "Y'all wanna hear somethin' to trip y'all out though? That nigga Money Mike hit one of my people up talkin' 'bout he wants me to sit down with the bitch to settle our differences. Can you believe that shit?"

The group chuckled as Dre sat in disbelief.

"I mean, that nigga got me all fucked up with that shit," he said. "If we end that bitch tonight, can we get in to pop the other one laid up in the hospital?"

"I know for a fact Money doesn't like that bitch," Ritchie said. "As soon as Sharice is gone, we're gonna be able to whack that broad with no problems."

"Fuckin' hired guns. Had one job to do, and couldn't do it. Got the nerve to wanna be high priced and shit," Dre said. "It don't matter though. If that bitch shows up at the spot, we gonna take care of that shit. Tell you what, any nigga that can catch the bitch alive, I'm puttin' up thirty g's. I wanna be the one to cap that bitch myself."

"Thirty large for catchin' that broad? Oh count me in, nigga," J Rock said as he dapped Dre. "I'll ride on them tonight and make sure she don't have a scratch on her."

"For sure. I'm gonna make sure I take her ass out slow, on the real," Dre said with a wicked grin on his face. "Ritchie, let my cousin know where he's goin' so he can roll through. We gonna celebrate once this bitch is done."

Dre and the others all dapped each other as the crew members made their way back to their cars. As Ritchie made his way over towards Lil Dee, he received a text from Bull asking to meet up with him. Ritchie texted back asking for a location before meeting up with Lil Dee.

A few hours later, Sharice was sitting at a local coffee shop with Jerome being very cautious as she looked around the area since the two were sitting at an outside table. Jerome chuckled as he watched his lover be overly cautious. It's a modern coffee shop close to the river and had an abundance of tourist and police presence in the area. Sharice noticed Jerome laughing at her.

"Oh, I see you got jokes?" Sharice said with a cryptic smile.

"I mean, come on, Kiss. Half the police force is here, and you still all nervous and shit," he responded.

"Niggas who want to get you will get you no matter who's around," Sharice replied before she took a quick sip of her drink. "I mean, I didn't think someone would have the heart to try and pop me in my damn club with FBI surveillance on my ass, but the bullet the hospital removed from Connie said otherwise."

Jerome nodded his head with understanding. He can tell Sharice was still hurting because of that incident.

"Sorry, Reese. I didn't mean to make light of the shit you goin' through," Jerome said. "I just was tired of being cooped up in the house or that damn club. Just wanted to be out in the real world with you, especially on a beautiful day like this."

Sharice smiled as she lowered her guard for a moment.

"I guess it's nice to be out," Sharice admitted. "I mean, you know how my paranoid ass is."

"Oh, I know," Jerome said with a chuckle. "I mean, normally niggas who smoke weed are paranoid as fuck. Your ass is so fuckin' paranoid, that you won't smoke because it makes you paranoid!"

Sharice was confused because Jerome was making no sense to her, but shrugged it off as she continued with her drink. The couple's moment was short lived when Sharice's phone suddenly rang. She took one more sip of her drink before she answered the call.

"Yeah... okay... Is everything set to go? Alright... okay... I'm on my way," she said before she hung up.

"Well, it's that time," she said to Jerome who nodded his head.

"Be careful, Kiss," Jerome said as Sharice leaned over and shared a kiss with him.

"I got this. boo," she said before she rose from her seat and walked off towards her car.

Just inside the uptown area of the city, there were a series of old, boarded-up, supposedly abandoned warehouse buildings. The area was pretty quiet with the only sound coming from a nearby main road faintly heard through the area. Uncut grass filled the area, making it hard to see throughout the block, with a huge water-filled canal located at the back of the main warehouse.

Lil Dee was sitting a block down from the targeted warehouse in his car, shaking his head, still upset over being assigned the task of staking out the building. He almost dozed off when the sight of a black SUV pulling up outside the warehouse caught his attention. He watched as he noticed Sharice exiting from the SUV. His eyes lit up as he quickly located his cell phone.

Inside the run-down warehouse, was the eighteen-wheeler Michelle and James had stolen earlier. They were both overseeing a few other crew members who were unloading the truck when Sharice walked in and approached them.

"Hey, are we on schedule?" she asked.

"Just finished the last load right now," Michelle said as she walked over with a duffle bag and checked out her boss' outfit. "A little overdressed, aren't we?"

Sharice rolled her eyes as Michelle opened the duffle bag to reveal the euros they uncovered when they stole the rig.

"I didn't know if you expected this or not,"

Michelle said.

Sharice nodded her head as Michelle zipped the bag up.

"I figured as much. These assholes deal with overseas a lot too, so I thought there was a possibility. Actually, works in our favor," Sharice said. "What about that other thing? Is that being handled?"

"As far as we know," James said. "That was the x-factor in all this."

Sharice nodded her head as she pulled out her cell phone and made a call as a hint of concern filled her eyes.

A little less than an hour had passed as darkness filled the area with the night upon the city. Several cars pulled up next to Lil Dee's car, which was still parked a block down from the main warehouse, filled with soldiers all armed with guns. J Rock walked up to Lil Dee, who rolled down the car window.

"They still in there," he asked.

"As far as I know. I saw a couple of SUVs enter the building, and no other niggas came out. But that SUV right there, the black one, that's the shit ol' girl pulled up in so I know she's up in there," Lil Dee reported.

J Rock nodded his head as he waved his crew forward.

"Keep a watch out, hit me on the cell if you see anythin'," J Rock told Lil Dee before he himself walked off.

J Rock smiled as he and his crew made their way to the main warehouse. He licked his lips as he looked forward to filling his blood rage.

Chapter 8

Endgame

It's mid-day and a nice weather day on the lakefront as the calming water was soothing for those who were in the area. Sharice was sitting quietly on a nearby bench, her eyes covered with her shades as she gazed at the lake water almost in a trance. Her mood was short lived as Money's limo stopped on the curb. He hopped out, approaching her with a scowl on his face.

He walked over, expecting a greeting from her, but she didn't budge. Sharice just continued to gaze upon the lake in silence.

"What the fuck, Sharice?" he said, waiting for an

explanation. "I walk over here, and you don't even say shit?"

"I'm here cause you asked me here," Sharice responded almost in a monotone way. "So, what is it that you need?"

"What do I need? How about some answers," Money snapped back. "All this fuckin' shit that went on a few days ago. I told you not to do a fuckin' thing! And what do you do? What the fuck did you do?!"

Sharice was unbothered as she slowly removed her sunglasses from her face. She looked towards Money with a hint of disrespect in her eyes.

"I don't know what you're talking about," she calmly said before she turned her attention back towards the lake.

******

Days prior, Sharice walked out of the bathroom of the club looking like a million bucks from head to toe as Tracy, who was sitting at the bar looking through her phone, looked up and started whistling as she admired her boss. She was wearing a tight, strapless blue tube dress, which rode up to her thighs, with matching blue strapless heels with her toes and nails polished to perfection.

"Alright, girl. I see you," she said playfully as Sharice approached her. "I see you tryin' to leave this date married for real."

Sharice giggled before she took a seat on a stool next to her friend.

"So, where y'all going?" a nosey Tracy asked.

"He wants to take me out to some café. Nothing flashy," Sharice answered.

"Lookin' like that? Girl, you dressed like you goin' to the Oscars or something," Tracy said with a smile. "You are overdressed, boo."

"I know, but shit, it's not like I get to go out a lot," Sharice responded. "This the first time we're like really out. Not in a restaurant, or in each other's spot, but like out in the open and shit. I wanna turn a few heads, including his."

"Well, I wouldn't be surprised if he doesn't try and cancel the date and meet you at the Rochambeau, for real," Tracy said while she laughed.

Sharice chuckled as well as she took out her phone to check the time.

"You really think I'm overdressed?" she asked her friend.

"For a café date? Yes. If it was me, I'd tone it down slightly," Tracy answered.

"Well, do me a favor, go pick me out something real quick that's café worthy, please," Sharice asked.

"So, now I gotta lay your clothes out for you?" Tracy mocked when Sharice's cell phone started to ring.

"Please, Trace," Sharice begged as Tracy rolled her eyes and stood up from her stool.

"Fine, fine. It'd be worth it just to get you outta here for the day," she said before she walked off.

Sharice chuckled as she looked at her cell phone. She didn't recognize the number and was about to ignore the call, but decided to pick up the line after several rings.

"Hello?" Sharice said, surprised to hear the collect call message with Diego's name attached to it.

She looked confused as she pressed one on the phone to receive the call.

"Diego?"

"Hey, yeah. Look, I'm really in a bind right now, Sharice," Diego said. "They picked me up talkin' about obstruction of justice and shit. They know about me and you meeting up and everything. I need some help, Sharice."

Sharice was stunned as she pondered for a moment, choosing her words wisely.

"I don't know what you're talkin' 'bout," she answered. "If you're in trouble, you should contact a lawyer for help, not me."

"Sharice! I don't have money for a lawyer," a

frustrated Diego said. "I put my life on the line for you, and they're talking about twenty years or more! Now... now, I need you to do whatever it is you do to make shit like this go away!"

"Diego, like I said, I don't know what you're talkin' 'bout. I can recommend a... a... hang on a second," Sharice said as a thought struck her mid-conversation.

A smile entered her face as she went back to the line.

"Hey, check it out. I'll take care of the lawyer for you, no problem. Where are you being held?" Sharice asked as she quickly located some paper and a pen behind the bar at the register.

Diego gave her the specifics as she wrote down the information quickly before going back to the line.

"Okay, hang tight. I'm gonna get someone over there within the hour," she said before she hung up the line.

She quickly looked through her contacts and called her lawyer, giving him specific instructions. After a few moments, she hung up the line as Tracy returned with an outfit for Sharice.

"Hey, this is the best you have in the closet," she said as Sharice rose from her seat.

"Hey, my bad, I have to go. I don't have time to change right now. I'll bring some more outfits to stock up in a few days," she responded.

"Or, you could actually live at your home like normal folks," Tracy quipped.

Sharice shot her a look before she made her way out of the club. Tracy sighed as she headed back up to the office to return the outfit she had selected back into the closet.

In the Federal lock-up facility, about forty-five minutes later, Diego was led into a cold interrogating cell to meet with Sharice's lawyer. Asher, who was an older Jewish man, was wearing an expensive suit and looking over Diego's file when his client arrived. Diego was handcuffed to the table as the officer walked out of the room.

"Mr. Diego Castillo, I presume," Asher asked.

"Yes."

"My name is Asher Fuks. I'll be representing you with your case on behalf of Ms. Legget," he said as he shook Diego's hand. "Now, I have some good news, and I have some bad news, and I need you to pay attention, as time is of the essence."

Diego nodded his head with understanding.

"If this thing goes to trial, you will lose," Asher continued, shocking Diego.

"What?"

"The federal government has a ninety-five percent conviction rate, Mr. Castillo, which means they aren't in the business of losing," he responded. "In fact, they could have pulled you long before the obstruction charge they tacked on. You were an asset to leave in the real world, but when you endangered one of their own, they took it personal."

Diego looked defeated as he covered his face in

shame.

"Oh my god," he responded as Asher tried to comfort him.

"However, there are other ways we can do this," Asher responded. "They are going to ask the judge for the full twenty-year sentence if we go to trial. Plead guilty, and it'll probably drop down to twelve years."

"What the fuck?! I can't go to jail for twelve years! I have a wife and kids to support," Diego responded, and Asher once again tried to calm his new client down.

"You didn't let me finish," Asher calmly said. "Twelve years is if you plead guilty. If you offer them something, that twelve could be knocked down to, let's say, seven, maybe less."

Diego was confused by Asher's suggestion.

"You want me to snitch?" he asked. "Why would you offer that? Aren't you Sharice's lawyer?"

"I am," Asher responded. "She's not the one you're going to inform on. If you agree to this, your family will be taken care of for as long as you're away. Once you are released, there will be an account waiting for you with five hundred thousand dollars deposited. With that, you could start a new life. Like I said, time is of the essence. If you want this deal, let me know now or take your chances with the public attorney. And before you say it, I know what you're thinking, you could inform on my client because it's your right to do so, which is true. Of course, I couldn't be involved in that, and would you really want me to tell her that's the route you chose to go down when the goal is to keep your family safe?"

Diego sighed as he slowly shook his head. Asher nodded his head as he looked at Diego once more.

"So, Mr. Castillo, what's it going to be?"

Diego sighed once again because jail frightened him. He knew he's vulnerable right now and had no other choice but to take Sharice up on her offer.

"Fine, I'm in," he struggled to say.

Asher nodded his head as he and Diego begin to discuss what he needed to do to satisfy Sharice's *request.*

About an hour later, Diego, Asher, Davis, and Daniels were all sitting in the interrogation room together negotiating Diego's sentence amongst themselves. Asher looked at his phone when it showed a text. He read the text, which said 'it's a go' on it, and put his phone back into his pocket.

"Gentlemen, are we going to do this or what?" Asher asked. "My client has valuable information that can better help you and your bureau rid the streets of a sizable amount of illegal substances. For that cooperation, we're willing to accept five years, but it has to be now."

"Five years? For police corruption?" an amazed Daniels said. "No way he gets off that easy."

"Agent Daniels, we're talking about an illegal substance bust with the street value of over fifteen million dollars! Think of the headlines, and funding that will increase with this bust," Asher responded.

"But he can't tell us where he got the information from, or who's bringing it in," Daniels snapped back. "Right now, we're just talking about hearsay."

"The deal is going on at this very moment. If we wait any longer, it'll be done, and you, Agent Daniels, will look like the fool who let fifteen million dollars go on the street quibbling over a difference of five years, and letting who knows how many perps continue to walk on the street. Think of how that headline will look," Asher responded, giving Daniels something to think about.

"Seven years," Daniels responded.

"Six years," Asher replied.

Daniels looked at Davis, who nodded his head with agreement.

"Fine, six years," Daniels said in agreement. "Now, where is the drop going to be?"

"You must not think too highly of me, Agent Daniels," Asher mocked. "We need this on paper, and again, we need to do this quickly. Once we have the agreement in writing, and only then, will my client reveal what he knows."

Daniels frowned as he turned his attention to Davis and nodded his head. Davis quickly made his way out of the interrogation room to get the federal attorney.

Later that night, Lil Dee was sitting silently in his car from a distance overlooking the targeted warehouse observing J Rock and his crew all make their way to the building in question. He watched as they all snuck in the back door of the warehouse out of his view.

Once in the building, J Rock and his soldiers heard music playing towards the center of the massive building. There were a bunch of boxes and other discarded materials in the building with cobwebs filled the surroundings as well. All of J Rock's crew had their guns drawn and pointed as they quietly made their way towards the music, which got louder and louder as they approached.

Everyone was on pins and needles as they tiptoed, trying not to make a sound. J Rock noticed the eighteen-wheeler Michelle and James had stolen in the building. He cautiously walked over towards the truck where there was a Bluetooth speaker and phone that was playing the music. One of J Rock's crew was about to stop the music when J Rock stopped him, motioning him and another soldier to open up the back of the trailer connected to the rig.

He motioned for the rest of his crew to aim towards the trailer as they cautiously waited for the doors to open. Everyone was in position as J Rock gave the nod to open the trailer's doors. The doors are quickly opened and everyone was on edge.

J Rock looked in the trailer and noticed a bloody body leaned up against a stack of canisters. He and a few others entered the trailer, which was about a third empty and approached the body, which was full of blood with a mask covering its face. J Rock removed the mask and was stunned to discover Ritchie's lifeless body with several gunshot wounds throughout his body.

"What the fuck?" he said, confused when his cell phone began to vibrate.

He checked the caller ID and noticed it's Lil Dee calling.

"Yeah, what is it?" J Rock said as he struggled to hear due to the loud music playing in the area. "What? I can't hear you. Hold on a second."

J Rock turned to one of the soldiers next to the radio as he hopped out of the trailer.

"Aye, turn that shit off," he said.

The soldier quickly turned off the music as J Rock went back to the phone.

"Yeah, what you were sayin'?" he asked.

Lil Dee was ducked down hidden in his car as several police vehicles sped past his car, closing in on *the warehouse.*

"Nigga, I said the police are headin' your way. That bitch set us up! Get the fuck outta there now," he said before he quickly hung up his phone.

J Rock was stunned as he slowly lowered his phone. Before he could react, a smirk entered his face as he dropped his phone on the ground.

"We've been fucked," he said to his crew.

Everyone was confused until the front and back doors of the warehouse burst open with federal agents and local cops all entering the building with their guns drawn. The authorities were yelling to J Rock and his crew to drop their weapons, which some of the crew did immediately. The others looked towards J Rock, who was considering going out in a blaze of glory, but at the last minute, he decided to surrender his weapon as well. The rest of the crew followed his lead. Several officers ran over and slammed J Rock and his crew down, one by one, before they placed the cuffs on each individual.

About an hour after the bust, Daniels and Davis arrived at the warehouse and made their way towards the big rig. They looked at the product that had been pulled from the trailer and the body bag with Ritchie's body. Daniels walked over to the agent who was logging the contents as evidence.

"Any problems?" Daniels asked.

"No, not a single shot was fired," the agent answered.

"Who's in the body bag?"

"We're not sure yet, but the body was here when we arrived. We're trying to get an ID on him as we speak," the agent answered.

"So, how much dope are we talking here?" Davis asked.

"Well, it's definitely not fifteen million," the agent responded, disappointing both Daniels and Davis. "No, this is more like twenty-one or twenty-two million dollars, give or take."

Daniels was stunned as he and Davis shared a look,.

"One hell of a bust, sir. This one is going to gain some attention as one of the biggest busts ever on US soil," the agent said before she walked off.

Davis patted Daniels on the back, congratulating him, but Daniels wasn't satisfied.

"It's not what I wanted," Daniels said. "I know Sharice had something to do with this."

"Well, it's what we got," Davis responded. "Let's work over the crew and see what they can tell us. Maybe one of them will flip."

Daniels shook his head in disgust as both he and Davis made their way around the rest of the crime scene.

******

Sharice was sitting on the bench quietly on the lakefront as Money waited for an answer on the warehouse bust.

"So, you don't know anything about any of that shit?" he asked.

"Only what I saw on TV," Sharice responded. "What do you care for anyway? It's not like your politicians are gonna bitch about that. I mean, a multimillion-dollar drug bust? Enough to show the public that they're winning the war on drugs. Who wouldn't want that shit?"

Money backed away as he chuckled to himself.

"Aight, I'll give you that," he said as he took a seat next to her on the bench. "But I also heard Dre is nowhere to be found. I mean, with a lot of his crew locked up and shit, he suspiciously has gone missin'. What you got to say about that shit?"

Sharice shook her head and shrugged, once again playing the innocent role.

******

Two days prior, James and Michelle were sitting on the couch inside the apartment Michelle had observed Dre visiting several days earlier. They both had wool masks that were on top of their heads, but not covering their faces at the moment. Sharice, also with a wool mask on top of her face, exited the bathroom where the female Dre was seen with days earlier, was taped up and dead in the bathtub, seemingly strangled to death. Sharice was not her glamorous self, dressed in sweats and tennis shoes. The tension had her nervous as she began to pace.

"Fuck! Michelle, are you sure it was that nigga?" she asked. "Maybe it was some other fool that looked like him."

"Nah, it was him. I've seen that nigga a hundred times," Michelle responded. "You know we got this right, Reese? I mean, you don't have to be here for this shit."

"Yeah, Reese, why don't you take off? We got this shit handled for real," James said as Sharice looked at both of them strangely.

"I know y'all just tryin' to get me outta here so y'all can fuck," she responded, surprising both James and Michelle.

James looked at Michelle, stunned.

"You told her?" he asked.

"Look, it wasn't that big of a deal, damn," Michelle responded.

The two continued to go back and forth when they heard keys jiggling on the door lock. Sharice waved them quiet as she positioned herself just outside of the door's view behind a nearby wall. She pulled out her gun from her back belt and lowered her mask over her face. Michelle and James also quickly hid while lowering their masks as the door opened with Dre, who held a couple of bags of fast food items.

"Hey, baby girl, I got that new chicken sandwich niggas been fightin' for," he said.

Before he could close the door fully, he accidentally dropped one of the bags. As he reached down to pick it up, Sharice turned around the corner and fired a shot, missing Dre, catching him off guard. He quickly looked up, noticed Sharice, and quickly reached for his gun. Sharice fired another shot that hit him in the shoulder, causing him to drop his weapon on the ground. He quickly backed out of the apartment as Sharice continued to fire shots at him. After he exited the apartment, Dre suddenly tripped and fell down the stairs as Sharice walked above him with her gun drawn.

A bruised and bloodied Dre looked up towards Sharice in defeat as she aimed her gun right at him. He smiled as he took a deep breath.

"I know that's you under there," he said. "So what are you waiting for? Do it!"

Sharice didn't respond as Michelle and James both approached her, questioning what's going on.

"What the fuck? We gotta go," Michelle said as

Sharice relived Connie's shooting in her head repeatedly. She took a deep breath and looked Dre square in his eyes as he taunted her.

"Do it! Do it with your hoe ass! Do-"

Sharice fired two shots into Dre's head, killing him as she stood over him for several more moments. James quickly turned to Michelle.

"Look, go get the car. We then made too much noise and need to bounce, ya heard me," he said.

"What about the girl?" Michelle asked.

"Fuck that bitch, let's go!" James said as Michelle scurried off.

James turned his attention to Sharice, who was still looking at Dre's body, almost as if she was obsessed.

"Boss, you gotta go. You gotta get outta here," he softly said.

Sharice finally snapped out of her trance as Michelle made her way over with the car and popped the trunk, which has plastic laid out in it.

"Grab him," Sharice said as she reached down and

grabbed Dre's legs.

A confused James did as ordered as he grabbed Dre's top half. Michelle ran over and helped Sharice with his bottom half as they quickly carried him over to the car, dumping his body inside the trunk. Michelle quickly reached into the back seat of the car and pulled out several bottles of bleach. She handed one to James as the two of them quickly splashed bleach on all the blood-tainted areas on the ground. After the quick job, all three of them got in the vehicle and pulled off.

Sharice, who was sitting in the back seat, took off her mask, looking at the blood on her clothing. Michelle was already taking off her outfit when she noticed Sharice in a daze.

"Reese, come on! Snap out of it!" she said. "Take off them clothes!"

Sharice nodded her head as she began to strip out of her bloodied sweats. She handed the clothes over to Michelle, who placed them in a plastic garbage bag she had with her. A slight smirk entered Sharice's face. She *was filled with satisfaction killing her friend's attacker.*

******

Sharice leaned back on the bench and didn't say a word, which infuriated her boss.

"Where's he at, Reese? Huh? Did you kill him?" Money asked.

"No."

"The nigga is missin'. They went by his bitch house, and she's taped up and shit, dead in the tub, and they found some blood around the complex too. You tellin' me you ain't have nothin' to do with that?" Money asked once more.

"No, nigga," Sharice said. "You told me no violence, so I didn't do shit. I can follow instructions, for real. Unlike back in the day when you took out Atr-"

"Hey! What the fuck?!" Money snapped to a surprised Sharice. "We not talkin' about what I did!

We're talking about you. I know you killed that nigga, so just fuckin' say it. I'm not gonna be mad and shit. Be a real bitch and admit it!"

"I didn't kill him, okay!" Sharice fired back. "That nigga had plenty of enemies. Have you checked in on K-One's people? I mean, he did smoke they partna. Why are you sweatin' me?"

Money shook his head with frustration as Sharice decided to turn on the charm.

"Look, you said play nice; I played nice. I didn't have anything to do with none of that shit. Let's just be happy for the shit that did happen because it benefits us all around, ya heard me," Sharice said with a flirtatious smile on her face. "The feds got one of the biggest busts in US history, according to the TV, and Dre, who has been a pain in my ass, is fuckin' gone. Why are we worried about who did what, when we should be thankful that the shit storm is over with? Now, doesn't that sound a little better?"

Sharice re-crossed her legs, this time making sure

her leg was crossed over in-between Money's legs as she slightly cuddled up to him. Her flirtatious charm overwhelmed Money as he looked down at her smooth legs, wanting a taste so bad. Eventually, he slowly nodded his head with a smile on his face.

"You think you hot shit, don't you?" Money said as he moved in close to her.

"Baby, you have no idea," she responded as she backed away from him and rose from the bench. "Are we good?"

Money rose from the bench as well, taking one last look at her, almost in a trance from her beauty.

"Yeah, we good, baby girl. We need to hook up for dinner one night to go over some shit, but we good," Money replied, much to Sharice's satisfaction.

She walked over and kissed him on his cheek, making sure he felt her body pressed against his before she walked off with a cryptic smile on her face. Money licked his lips as he watched Sharice leaving, obsessed with her walk.

Sharice got into a nearby SUV where Michelle was waiting for her.

"So, how'd that go?" Michelle asked.

"Had the nigga so hard he'll probably fuck one of them pelicans," Sharice said with a smile, causing Michelle to laugh. "Niggas can't think straight when that blood rushes to their dick. It's fuckin' crazy when you think about it."

Michelle nodded as she started the vehicle.

"So, it's over? We're in the clear," she asked.

"Nah, one more thing I gotta take care of," Sharice said while she buckled her seat belt. "I know you've been outta practice and shit, but how's that sniper trigger finger?"

Michelle looked at Sharice strangely, causing her to chuckle as the SUV pulled off down the street.

Later that night, at the docks, Alejandro and a few of his crew were patiently waiting as Sharice pulled up alone in her SUV. The area was isolated from the rest of the busy docks. Very faint light filled the area, which was a perfect atmosphere for a secret meeting.

Sharice exited out of her SUV and popped the trunk before she pulled out two large duffle bags. Alejandro and his crew were cautious as Sharice approached them, struggling slightly with the bags.

"Well, it's nice to see that chivalry isn't dead in Columbia," Sharice said sarcastically as she dropped the bags at Alejandro's feet.

He smiled as he looked at her.

"Thank you for meeting me," he said. "It's always nice when people work with us, instead of us having to kill their family members to get their attention."

"Well, I don't have any of that, so I'm good," Sharice quipped back. "In the bags is what I owe you."

Alejandro slowly reached down and opened one of the bags, checking out the money bonded together. Alejandro was impressed as he zipped up the bag.

"Euros?" he asked.

"Yep. There's two million euros there. Latest exchange has it around two point two million dollars. That's what you were owed and then some. We should be good," Sharice said.

"There's still the business of my dead man," Alejandro reminded Sharice. "Someone still has to answer for that."

"No, they don't," Sharice fired back, surprising Alejandro. "You see, I'm not stupid. You didn't come here to take him back or whatever bullshit excuse you told me before. I think you came here to kill him yourself for fuckin' up."

Alejandro chuckled as he looked impressed.

"You seem to have everything figured out," he said.

"Nah, I just know the type. Your story was bullshit. I could tell from the start. I know how you Columbian niggas work," she responded. "But, if it really means that much to your bosses to lose a nigga who fucked up and compromised the load, I have a proposition. I know you know who I roll with, right?"

Alejandro nodded his head as he motioned a couple of his men over to collect the bags.

"We've been havin' some supply issues. Our connect in Mexico has been fuckin' up a bit, so we may be in the market for a new supplier. Now, I ain't promisin' shit 'cause I gotta go back and talk with my people, but I'm sure we can get together and discuss a rate. I'm sure your cartel bosses wouldn't mind hookin' up with us."

Alejandro pondered for a moment as he talked to one of his crewmembers in their native tongue. After their discussion, he turned his attention back towards Sharice.

"So, you're looking to do business with us now?" he said with a cynical smile.

"Why not?" Sharice responded. "This time though, I'll be handling the shipment coming in the port. No more incompetence. We do the shit right, and we make money. What do you think?"

Alejandro pondered for a few moments. He nodded eventually in agreement.

"I have to bring it back to my bosses, but I'm sure we can work something out," he said as he and Sharice shook hands.

"I'll do the same," she said as she began to walk off.

"Hey, so are you going to tell me who killed our man?" Alejandro asked.

Sharice turned and smiled at Alejandro before continuing towards her SUV. Alejandro shook his head and chuckled to himself.

"Right," he said before he motioned his men back towards their vehicles.

Sharice looked up towards an adjacent building and waved her hand slightly to signal Michelle, who was peering out of a window, looking into a sniper riflescope observing the area. She noticed Sharice's signal and lowered her rifle as she packed her gear up.

Later that night, the normally crowded Club Exotica was a shell of itself, emptied without a single soul in sight with the exception of Tracy, who was sitting behind the bar surfing on her cell phone. An exhausted Sharice entered the club with Michelle by her side when she noticed her friend sitting behind the bar. She had a few parting words with Michelle, before she approached her friend. She took a seat at the barstool across from her.

"Hey, what you doin' here?" Sharice asked.

"I still get paid by the hour, you know that right?" Tracy responded as she put her cell phone away. "Even if we're not open."

"Well, fuck, you could have taken the night off and got paid. I would have still hooked you up. I mean, with all the shit that's gone down, you deserve a break," Sharice said as Tracy went behind the bar and fixed both of them a drink.

"Yeah, I feel you. I still can't get over Connie being shot," Tracy responded. "Have you been to see her?"

Sharice nodded her head as she took a sip of her drink.

"I was there for a little bit, but she was still unconscious," she responded.

"Well, she's awake now," Tracy responded. "Crazy thing was all she was doing was asking about you. Was you good and stuff. I'm like bitch, you're in the hospital after being shot. She didn't seem to care. Typical Connie."

Sharice didn't respond much as she took a few more sips of her drink. Tracy noticed her friend had something on her mind.

"Reese, you okay?" she asked.

"Yeah, it's just... Trace, Connie did some bad shit. I mean, some really bad shit. I was fuckin' done with the girl, I swear to Christ, but then she saved my life. I've been just going round and round with this shit ever since it happened," Sharice admitted.

"Any way you can tell me what she did to piss you off?" Tracy asked.

Sharice sighed before she shook her head, refusing.

"It's one of those business things, ya know," Sharice responded. "Just know she fuckin' hurt me real bad, and I should be done with her altogether."

"So, you feel since she saved your life, you owe her?" Tracy deduced.

"I mean, yes she did save me, but it still doesn't change the fact that she did what she did to me," Sharice answered. "How can I let that shit go? I was so fuckin' pissed at her. I was ready to cut all ties with her, and then this shit happened. Before the shooting, I didn't give a fuck one way or another about what happened to her. After she was shot, all I could think about was... was-"

"That you wanted her to live," Tracy finished.

Sharice nodded her head before finishing off her drink.

"You and Connie then been through a lot together," Tracy explained. "I mean, whatever happened between you two, you still had history together. You shouldn't feel bad about that. I mean, we just lost Lavina not too long ago. Losing two close friends, no matter the circumstances, is hard."

Sharice sighed. Her loyalty to Lavina still had her doubting her feelings for Connie.

"I don't think it will ever be the same," Sharice admitted. "No matter what, I don't know if I could ever trust Connie again even after this shooting. I just... I just don't know."

"It doesn't have to be the same," Tracy replied. "I mean, you can still appreciate her for what she did, and still keep your distance if needed. Yeah, she saved you, but Connie is still who she is. Saving your life isn't gonna change all that. I'm just sayin' you don't have to forget and forgive, but you can still show your gratitude, or whatever it is you think you need to show. Through it all, she's still your homegirl. I bet whatever she did to you, had somebody else did the same thing, you would have handled it totally different, am I right?"

Sharice nodded her head, agreeing with her friend's words. She knew if anyone else would have killed Lavina, she would have killed them without question. Showing Connie mercy was outside the norm for her.

"See. There's still feelings for her inside you," Tracy pointed out. "You showed her favor. That means there still is love for the girl. It can be repaired as time goes on, but you don't have to kiss her ass right now just because she saved you."

Sharice chuckled as Tracy finished her drink.

"Go see her, Reese. Talk. It won't fix all, but it's a start," Tracy advised.

"I'll think about it," Sharice responded. "I swear, I should be payin' you by the hour," Sharice commented.

"You already are," Tracy pointed out with a smirk.

"It's just you should be paying me more by the hour."

"Bitch, I just gave you a raise," Sharice fired back. "Damn, can you at least get your first check before asking for another one?"

"See, now that was spoken like a true businesswoman. Well, not with the profanity and all, but we can work on that," Tracy quipped, causing her friend to smile.

After a few moments, Sharice sighed as she looked around the club.

"So, when are we opening back up?" she asked.

"It's up to you, boss. Police have canvassed the area and got all they needed. I just wanted to wait for you to give me the word. Had a few contractors come in this evening and patch up the bullet holes, so I'm good to go whenever you are," Tracy responded.

"Tomorrow it is," Sharice said. "Kinda glad we're closed tonight. Nice and quiet. Can finally get some sleep."

"I know you can, at your house," Tracy responded.

"Come on, Trace, I don't wanna go home! I got work to do and-"

"And nothing! Sharice, this isn't a fuckin' hotel! Take your ass home! Call Rome, get you some dick, and shut the fuck up," Tracy snapped, surprising her friend.

"Shit, I think I like the G-rated you better," Sharice said as she rose up from her barstool. "Swear to God, I thought I was the boss here, and you were the employee."

"I'm not tellin' you as an employee, I'm tellin' you as a friend," Tracy said with a smile.

"Well, as your boss, I'm takin' your raise back," Sharice joked as she began to walk off.

"Don't play with my money," Tracy yelled only to receive a middle finger from her friend as she exited the club.

Chapter 9

Epilogue

The next night, an exhausted Sharice was lying in her bed, breathing heavily next to Jerome, who embraced her from behind after the two had finished having one of their sexual encounters. Jerome kissed her neck softly, causing his lover to giggle.

"Stop it," she playfully said as Jerome pulled her in close.

"Seems like you had some stress you needed to work out tonight," Jerome said, causing her to giggle once more.

"Yeah, it's been a crazy week," Sharice said. "I'm just glad this shit is over, you know."

"Me too. I don't like my ol' lady on them streets battlin' niggas and shit," Jerome said.

"Oh, so I'm your ol' lady now?"

"Better be at this point, shit," he replied with a laugh. "I'm just ready to get away to Houston to put in this work. I think it'll be nice to spend some more time together, for real."

Sharice's smile slowly faded from her face as she turned around and faced her lover.

"About that, I've been meaning to tell you," Sharice started off. "I got with Rico, and told him I'm out on Houston."

A disappointed Jerome was shocked by Sharice's decision.

"Why? Why would you not do this shit," he asked.

"I just got too much goin' on out here. I mean, Connie is laid up in the hospital, I have all new territory I need to get straight, plus the other deal I brokered. It's just… it's not the right time to do this. Not for me," Sharice explained. "I mean, I can still talk him into lettin' you ride on it. It's just, I can't do it right now."

Sharice could tell her words disappointed her lover. He took a moment to think but eventually nodded his head, agreeing.

"You gotta do what you gotta do," he said, causing Sharice to smile once more. "Well, since I'm not going to Houston without you, how about we talk about me crewin' up with you and yours?"

Once again, the smile slowly faded from Sharice's face as confusion took its place.

"Crewin' up?" she asked. "What are you talkin' bout?"

"I wanna be down with you and yours," Jerome clarified. "I think it's time you add me on, boss."

Jerome could tell that Sharice wasn't feeling his plan.

"Is that a problem?" he asked.

"Rome, I don't think that's a good idea," Sharice said.

"Why not?"

"Well, I need a regular guy for a relationship, not someone who works for me," Sharice answered to a confused Jerome.

"I work for you now?" he replied.

"You know what I mean. I can't work with someone on a daily basis that I'm supposed to be attached to. How would that look?" she asked.

"It would look like you and me were a couple," Jerome answered. "What's wrong with that?"

"What's wrong with it is I have to maintain discipline and order," Sharice responded. "How can I do that when everyone would undermine me because they think I'm givin' you preferential treatment and shit?"

"Who cares what them niggas think? Me and you would know what's goin' on," Jerome said. "I mean, you was just about to spend a couple of months or whatever the fuck in Houston together. This is the same shit."

"No, it isn't," Sharice corrected. "First, it was only temporary. Two, maybe three months at the most. Second, that was before all of this. I wasn't plannin' on hookin' back up and shit, and if I had known I was, I wouldn't have even thought about bringing you on that job."

"Why not?"

"Because Jerome, you're my weakness," Sharice finally admitted. "You are my heart, and if niggas out there knew that, they would come for you to hurt me. The more people see us outside together, the more they'll learn how to take advantage of it. If you were part of the crew, they would know. Everyone would know."

Jerome looked on like he was offended by his lover's words. He got out of bed and began to get dressed, much to Sharice's surprise.

"Can't believe this shit," he said. "You makin' it seem like I'm some hoe ass nigga that can't handle my shit! Like I can't handle shit out in the streets! I've been on the block for a minute now, and I ain't scared of no nigga, ya heard me."

"Rome, please, that's not what I'm sayin'," Sharice pleaded with him. "I know you can handle things and all, it's just all about appearance right now. You are my weakness, for real, but another thing is with you by my side, these niggas will never respect me. They'd think it's all about you and make me look like a fuckin' afterthought. You know that!"

"Yeah, same shit different day," Jerome said, sitting on the bed put on his shoes.

Sharice moved over close to him and hugged him from behind with tears flowing down her face.

"Bae, please," she said softly. "Don't go."

Jerome softened his stance as he held Sharice's hands that were crossed on his chest.

"Maybe you're right," he said. "I mean, look at this shit. If we woulda been trippin' like this, and then had to go out in public, them niggas would be lookin' at us all crazy and shit."

"Workplace romances don't never work," Sharice said as Jerome turned to her.

He wiped the tears from her eyes as the two shared a kiss once more. After a few moments, Jerome backed away from her and rose from the bed.

"I don't know if this situation is gonna work out, Reese," he said. "Not while you're out there chasin' the dream and shit."

Sharice slowly nodded her head. As much as she hated to hear that, it was the best thing for her. She loved Jerome and enjoyed her time with him, but as long as she was out there chasing her dream to be boss, the two could never have a normal relationship in her eyes.

"Yeah. I was thinking the same thing," she responded. "You were right all along about this shit. I tried Rome, I really did. You are still my weakness though, and forever will be. I... I love you so fuckin' much."

Jerome sighed before he reached up and pulled

Sharice up from the bed as they looked at each other eye to eye.

"This damn life of ours," Jerome said with a smirk.

"One day, we can do this shit the right way. You know, actually date and shit. Not havin' to worry about a nigga knockin' our heads off," Sharice joked.

"Yeah, one day," Jerome said before sharing a kiss with his lover. "Maybe."

Jerome winked at Sharice before he walked out of her bedroom. Sharice seemed heartbroken but held her emotions in. She knew she was the cause of this, but it was the right call for her for the moment. She sat back on her bed and looked towards the side of the bed Jerome was laying on. She leaned over and took a whiff of his essence, still lingering on the sheets, which put a smile on her face.

There was a loud knock outside Money's expensive uptown home, which was decked out with a lot of expensive technology, artwork, and fixtures filling out the home comparable to Money's ego.

The loud knock continued as Money, still half asleep, slowly made his way towards the front door.

"Aight, I'm comin' muthafucka, damn!" Money yelled out as he finally made it to the door.

When he opened the door, Agents Daniels and Davis were there to greet him much to his disgust.

"Aw shit, what the fuck," he said before Davis grabbed him and slammed him up against the wall.

"Hello, Mike," Daniels said as his partner handcuffs the Faction boss.

"Man, this is some bullshit," Money said as Davis pats him down.

"Let's have a chat, shall we," Daniels said as both he and Davis led Money out of his home.

Money was being held in the FBI interrogation room with one wrist handcuffed to the table as Daniels, Davis, and Agent Flores were all in the room listening to a taped recording of Money and Sharice's conversation from the lakefront earlier that day. Daniels had a file he was looking over in his hand as he shook his head in disgust. Money looked around in confusion as Davis stopped the tape.

"Well?" Daniels said.

"Well, what?" Money responded. "I did what the fuck I could for y'all. I did exactly what you told me to!"

"Why don't you cut the bullshit!" Daniels yelled as he pulled several photos from the file and slammed them on the table. Money looked them over and noticed they were snapshots of him and Sharice sitting on the bench at the lakefront with her leg crossed over his, and another shot of Sharice kissing him on his cheek with her body pressed close to his.

Money shrugged it off, still confused.

"Okay, what's that shit supposed to mean?" he asked.

"Are you fucking with me?" Daniels asked. "You were supposed to get Sharice on the tape talking about the murder of Andre Brown, or being involved with the recent drug bust, or fucking anything we can use in court! You came in here with nothing but bullshit!!"

"Aye, I fuckin' tried, aight! I tried to get the shit outta her, but she's all secretive and shit! You heard the tape," Money explained.

"Davis, take a note," Daniels said. "Note that informant 6840 is not cooperating as part of his deal he struck with the government and is subject for full prosecution."

"Done," Davis said as Money began to change his tune.

"Wait, hold up, hold up," he said. "Come on now, I've been good to y'all niggas for real? I then gave you all the shit with Rico, and when you told me to curb the violence on the block, I did that shit too!"

"Lot of good it did. Andre Brown is missing, and the girl he was allegedly dating was found in her apartment duct tapped and strangled," Davis said. "I mean, how can you not know anything going on in your own fucking organization?! I'm starting to think Sharice is the real boss, and you're just the fall guy!"

"Come on, man. I'm out here bustin' my ass for you," Money said. "I gave you shit! The shipment shit and-"

"Nothing on John Bianchi, or any of his connections in New York," Daniels said. "The shipment bust didn't get us Rico or any top-level Faction members. You're feeding us bullshit!"

"I'm givin' y'all quality shit, ya heard me," Money responded. "Come on, man. You know I'm way more valuable on the streets, for real. Give me some more time, please."

Davis and Daniels looked at each other as Flores continued to look on in silence. Davis nodded his head with approval as Daniels turned his attention towards his informant.

"You better step it up," Daniels warned. "Anymore bullshit like this, not only will I have you prosecuted, but I'll add an obstruction of justice charge just for the fuck of it! Davis, can you please get him the fuck out of here?"

Davis unlocked the cuff on Money's wrist, pulled him from his chair, and led him out of the interrogation room. Flores shook her head with a chuckle as she picked up the photos from the table.

"You realize what Sharice has done, don't you?" Flores said to Daniels. "She's insulated herself. She's made it to where only those who she trusts the most can hurt her. Mike was never going to be an asset. He's just the fall guy that Sharice made sure she separated herself from."

Daniels nodded his head as a hint of disappointment filled his face knowing Flores was right.

"Yeah, I'm starting to see that," he responded. "That's why I think it's time to check out her inner circle."

Daniels took out his cell phone, logged into his

secure email, pulled up a link, and showed it to Flores. It was a picture of Michelle in her military gear.

"Michelle Johnson's military file. You were right," he said as Flores checked out a few other items in the email.

"What the hell? It said she did six months?" Flores said, shocked. "I thought we ran her through the database?"

"We did," Daniels responded. "The problem is after Katrina, so many things got twisted with servers and such. You would think they would have fixed their records by now, but files still get lost 'til this day, which is why we couldn't locate her. The military keeps documentation on all of their personnel past and present, which is why they had the documents. She's only been with Sharice's crew for a short time, but it seems she's taken Constance's place as Sharice's most trusted associate. Maybe if we can get to her, we can get to Sharice."

Flores nodded her head with approval as Daniels put his phone back in his pocket.

"Sounds like a plan. Still, even though it didn't lead to much, I'm impressed," she said. "When you said you had a high-level informant, I didn't think it was a boss."

"Like you said, Money is a boss in name only it would seem," Daniels replied. "We're playing this tight to the chest, so not many people know about his involvement. He still may be useful down the stretch."

"Since you're entrusting me with this information, does that mean I'm sticking around?" Flores asked with a smile on her face.

"You've proven yourself out there. Yeah, we'd like to keep you around. Maybe get you to do some UC work on Rico himself. You may be burned out here, but Miami is a whole new ball game," Daniels said, exciting Flores.

Flores looked at the pictures of Money and

Sharice once more before she and Daniels both walked out of the interrogation room.

A restless Sharice walked into her office holding two luggage bags, which she laid on a nearby sofa. She kicked her heels off and was about to head over towards her desk when there was a knock at her door. Michelle entered the office and noticed the luggage on the sofa.

"I thought I saw you sneak in here with luggage and shit. Damn, you movin' in or somethin'?" she asked.

"Nah, I just... sometimes it's easier to sleep here. Don't tell Tracy 'cause I don't wanna hear her mouth," Sharice said as she moved the luggage off the sofa so that she and Michelle could take a seat.

"Let me guess, nigga problems?" Michelle said.

Sharice chuckled as she nodded her head.

"Wanna talk about it?"

Sharice took a deep breath before responding.

"Not really. I'm just over it," she said. "As long as I'm out here in the game chasin' shit, it'll never work out between me and anybody. There's just so much more shit I need to achieve, and being in a relationship... I mean, how would that look?"

"Like you normal," Michelle quipped back.

"Excuse me?"

"Come on, Reese. You have a dude who loves you and knows what you do for a livin'. You know how rare that shit is in our line of business?" Michelle responded. "I mean, what I wouldn't give to live out in the open like you do with my boo. If he knew what I did for real, he'd probably bounce, and honestly, I don't blame him."

"Yeah, but don't you fear that someone is gonna get wind of him and try and harm him to get to you?" Sharice asked.

"Sometimes, but I knew that shit when I signed on," Michelle answered. "We're always gonna have enemies. I mean, what are we gonna do, just not live our lives? Shit, it's easier for you because your dude is in the shit with you. There ain't no reason you shouldn't be with that fine ass man!"

Sharice shook her head in disagreement.

"I just don't wanna be the reason something happens to him. He's a distraction to me, Chelle, that can cause me to fuck up a lot of shit, and because of that, it would make me look weak," she explained.

"Naw, because you and Connie were tight," Michelle retorted. "She's in the game too, and outside of whatever the fuck y'all was beefin' over before the shootin', you still allowed her to remain tight with you."

"That's different."

"Is it though? Sounds to me like you're scared of commitment," Michelle fired back. "'Cause none of these excuses make any sense. On the real, I think you're afraid that Jerome would be enough. You're afraid that if he becomes enough that you won't wanna do this thing anymore, or lose your drive. You love him, but you really love the game and all that comes with it. You've made it to the top because you're obsessed with the game. You decided to choose this thing over him, which is all kinds of fucked up, to be honest, but the thing is, you can have them both, baby."

Sharice still wasn't convinced as she changed the subject.

"Anyway, what you hearin' out on the streets?" Sharice asked. "Any chatter on anything?"

"Shit's quiet right now. Nothing much going down with Dre gone and the warehouse bust," Michelle said before she snapped her fingers. "Oh shit! So one of them niggas who was picked up during that bust, J Rock, the Aryans fucked his ass up bad in lock up. Word is they stabbed that nigga sixty some times up in that bitch thinkin' he had somethin' to do with hijackin' that truck."

Sharice nodded her head with approval.

"So, they are buyin' it then?" she asked. "Nothin'

is leadin' back to us?"

"Yep, we're clear of that as far as I can tell," Michelle said with a smile on her face.

"Good. What about on the block? Any pro-Dre niggas still runnin' around out there?" Sharice asked.

"Some nigga named Danky, who was said to be plottin' on you with Dre. We ain't got to him yet, but we got folks on the streets lookin'. That nigga Lil Dee is missin' too, but he isn't much of a threat without Dre. Either way, by week's end, all them corners will belong to us. Lot of new territory, for real. Any idea who you gonna give them to?" asked Michelle.

"I assume you wanna be considered?" Sharice said as Michelle batted her eyes.

"Well, you know. I'm just sayin', I did do some shit here," Michelle replied.

"Alright. Once we see what we all have, I'll hook you, James, and Jerome up," Sharice said. "And Bull... damn. Have you heard from him?"

Michelle's mood changed as the once bright smile

quickly disappeared.

"Yeah, he's pretty fucked up Reese," Michelle said. "I went over to his spot, and this nigga was drunk as shit. He's... he's really in a bad place right now."

Sharice shook her head as she felt sorrow for her friend.

"I know. Havin' to kill your childhood friend... I... I couldn't do that even if I wanted," Sharice said. "Havin' him do it... it's my one regret through all of this. Give him some time. He'll bounce back. Keep an eye on it when you can though. Let me know if shit gets too crazy."

Michelle nodded her head as she rose from the sofa.

"Well, boss, I'm gonna go get my freak on, so I'll leave you here with your illustrious solitude," Michelle said.

"Let me guess, you and James?"

"Ya fuckin' right," Michelle said with a smile.

"For someone who has a man at home, you sure

doin' a lot of extracurricular fucking," Sharice said with a grin.

"Theo is my man, my love, and all that and will always be for as long as he shall have me. James, however, is a nigga with a dick down to his ankles. You can't tell me you ain't never had some side dick as long as you been doin' this?" Michelle said with a smirk.

"Dick is one thing, but I never would do that if I had a good man at the crib," Sharice said before her curiosity is piqued. "His dick is really that big?"

"Humongous, and you still have a good man, lady boss, so quit trippin'. Just pick up that phone and watch how quick he comes runnin' back," Michelle said.

Sharice chuckled, once again changing the subject.

"Anyways, stop by in the morning. I wanna go visit Connie when I get up," Sharice said. "Oh, and lock that door."

Michelle nodded her head and waved as she walked out of the office. Sharice quietly looked around the lonely solitude she's created for herself. With Michelle's words on her mind, she took out her cell phone and looked up Jerome's number. She was tempted to call him but ultimately decided against it as she walked over to her desk.

She went into her bottom desk drawer and pulled out a small blanket. She kicked her feet up on her desk as she's known to do, and reached for the remote on her desk that controlled her office functions. She pressed a button that shut off the lights and covered herself with the blanket, trying to finally get some sleep.

The next morning, Sharice was fast asleep in her office when there was a sudden knock on her door. After several follow up, knocks Sharice finally woke up as she quickly checked the time on her phone.

"I know you're in there! Wake your ass up!" Tracy

shouted from the other side of the door.

Sharice cringed as she walked over to the office door and opened it.

"What have I told you about sleeping in here?" Tracy preached.

"I had a rough night, Tracy, damn," Sharice said, trying to fully wake up. "Can you come back and fuss another time, please?"

"Can't, there's some white guy downstairs looking to get with you," Tracy responded. "Johnny from Atlanta he said."

Sharice perked up as she quickly wiped her face.

"Why the fuck didn't you say anything?" Sharice asked as she quickly ran over to her luggage.

"I literally just did," Tracy responded as Sharice pulled out several clothing items from her bag.

"Give me about ten minutes and send him up," she said to her friend as she quickly tried to get herself ready.

Tracy shook her head with a smile as she walked

out of the office.

Ten minutes later, Tracy led John into the office to a completely transformed Sharice who walked over and greeted John with a hug, kissing him on both cheeks.

"Did y'all want anything?" Tracy asked.

"I'm good. John?"

"Nothin' for me, hun. Thanks," he said as Tracy exited the office.

Sharice took a seat behind her desk as John took a seat across from her.

"Nice place you got here. Lot better than that one you had last time," he said.

"Yeah, Katrina fucked that one up. This one has a lot more space," Sharice responded. "So, what's up? I didn't know you were in town."

"Yeah, had some business with a couple of contractors. Figured I'd stop by and see how things were going," he responded. "I heard it's been a rough couple of weeks up here."

"Yeah, it was bad. For a moment, I didn't know if I was gonna make it," Sharice said.

"Never doubted you would," John responded. "I was a bit shocked you turned down the Houston job though. It was your chance to become, well you know."

Sharice chuckled as she leaned back in her chair.

"You can talk in here, it's safe," she said.

"Either way, you could have had everything you wanted. I mean, I assume it's something you still wanted, right," he asked.

"Yeah, it's the only thing I've ever wanted," Sharice replied. "But all kinds of shit was goin' on, and tack on to the fact that my homegirl is in the hospital after taking a bullet for me. I just couldn't leave with things the way they were."

"I can respect that. I mean, you did good by us on that Colombian deal," said John. "Maybe that'll be good enough to sway Rico's vote."

Sharice chuckled as she shook her head in disagreement.

"I seriously doubt it. He wasn't too happy when I broke the news to him. Guess he figured he woulda been in there if he wasn't waitin' on me," Sharice responded. "It's not my time right now. One day, it will be."

John smiled as he nodded his head with agreement.

"In the meantime, you can always work with me in Atlanta. I know I was always against that before, but look at what Money's got you doin'," John said to a surprised Sharice. "I mean, no offense, but he has you doin' all the work while he does stuggots. Besides, the finance is where it's at. Insulates you from that street shit and makes you a harder target to reach for the feds. So, what do you say? You wanna come over and make some real bread in Atlanta?"

Sharice laughed as she shook her head.

"Back in the day, I would have ran at the offer.

But like you said, you always were against the shit and forced me to deal with that fool. Now because of you, I then got complacent, and because of that, I'm all in on N.O. So, sorry, but my answer is fuck the falcons," Sharice fired back with a smile as she kicked her legs up on her desk. "I ain't no dirty bird baby, I'm a Saint. I'm New Orleans. I wouldn't know what to do with myself in Hotlanta. Nola is in my blood, John. It's all I really know, ya heard me."

"Yeah, I know," John said with a chuckle while admiring Sharice's legs. "I see you still like to kick those sexy legs on top of your desk like I showed you. How's that workin' out for you?"

"You tell me," a flirtatious Sharice said as she extended her legs.

John looked her over and laughed as he got up from his chair. Sharice rose as well as the two shared a hug with each other.

"Eventually, I'll get you over to my side," John said. "You'll come to your senses one day."

"Never that," Sharice said as she kissed John on both cheeks once again.

"Take care, hun," he replied as he made his way out of the office.

Sharice giggled as she took a seat back behind her desk and leaned back in her chair once again. She pondered all that she had been through these past few weeks. She remembered Harold, her long-time soldier, and friend, who was gunned down. She remembered putting a bullet in Dre's leg, which started the entire conflict.

Her most emotional thought was the loss of her friend Lavina and the shooting of Connie, which brought her once cheerfulness down. A thought of Jerome brightened her mood slightly, but knowing he wasn't there for her once again brought her mood down.

Sharice may have won the war, but the cost weighed heavy on her heart as she looked around her office. As always, Sharice closed her eyes and took a deep breath. When she opened her eyes, all the pain and hurt that filled them are gone as she rose from her chair and got ready to start her day.

Check out more great Eric Nigma readings at:

www.enigmakidd.com

To submit a manuscript to be considered, email us at submissions@majorkeypublishing.com

Be sure to LIKE our Major Key Publishing page on Facebook!